T0025338

Neon Hemlock Press
www.neonhemlock.com
@neonhemlock

© 2020 Caitlin Starling

Yellow Jessamine
Caitlin Starling

Cover Illustration by Robin Ha
Interior Illustration by Karla Yvette
Cover Design by dave ring

ISBN-13: 978-1-952086-03-8

Caitlin Starling
YELLOW JESSAMINE

Neon Hemlock Press

THE 2020 NEON HEMLOCK NOVELLA SERIES

NEON HEMLOCK

Yellow Jessamine

BY CAITLIN STARLING

To those harboring the weight of self-blame: may you bury it.

chapter one

Out in the harbor, the ship's masts burned. The fires had caught on the sails and tarred ropes first, then spread, taking root on the deck itself. From this distance, there was no sound, no heat. There was only the glinting of flame against the dark sheet of the water below, and five bodies standing on a balcony to mark its passing.

"A shame," one of the watchers said, packing his pipe with an idle hand. "But at least it wasn't one of the grain shipments, eh?"

The owner of the ship did not respond, eyes fixed only on the conflagration of two months of his income.

"We must hope," said Lady Evelyn Perdanu, the only woman among their number, small and slight and draped in mourning black, "that your *Orrery* does not bring plague back with it as well, Mr. Danforth."

The pipe-packer paled, almost imperceptibly in the dim light. "It certainly will not. My men—"

"Your men run a dismal ship, thanks to your stinginess," the owner of the burning ship snapped. "And if it took my men, whom I keep generously supplied with clean water despite the mounting expense—"

"Gentlemen," said the assembly's oldest member, Weyland Sing. His grey hair was cut into a soft, short wave atop his head and the lines creasing his dark skin spoke to years at sea before his current wealth and comfort. "We must also consider the possibility that this is not a sickness of common provenance. There may be another hand at work."

Evelyn watched him closely through the confines of her long veil. At night, with few lanterns set to light their balcony, it was hard to make out the sharper lines of facial features, but she could discern the set of every man's shoulders well enough. Nobody spoke, because nobody wanted to acknowledge what they all knew, had all known for five years now.

Delphinium was dying. The city was as good as dead.

Even if *The Orrery* returned with its grain and its salted fish and its citrus, it would only stave off the inevitable. The military coup that had shattered the Cenanthe Empire had also cut off the capital from all but the closest of its farmland. Naval officers still patrolled the great sea beyond the harbor where once Delphinium had taken in riches beyond imagining, but now they were just as likely to torch a ship as to escort it.

Or to poison its crew, perhaps.

Delphinium had been left to rot, as the last old bones of the government refused to capitulate. Around them, in client cities and far-flung colonies, the empire continued under its new masters, prospering. But from her perch on the balcony, Evelyn could only smell the stench of decay, the sickly-sweet deliquescence of pride, of money, of men.

She turned her attention back out to the burning ship, now a column of flame.

"My lady," Danforth said, at her elbow, hesitant but arrogant as he always was. "What word did your sailors aboard *The Verity* bring when they docked this afternoon?"

"Nothing of note," she said, wishing he would leave her be. She should never have spoken. Often, the men forgot that she was there. She was only a wealthy wraith of a woman, unmarked, respected only in the way that small boys respected the monsters lurking beneath their beds at night. All of them would have preferred her gone, but her company owned too many ships, and her coffers were the second richest of all assembled. She was invited as a matter of duty.

"They saw military ships at least once a week on their voyage, just as all of our ships have. Do you have reason to expect different?" She looked over at Danforth, with his thick sideburns, his rakishly combed hair, his fine waistcoat.

"Of course not," he said, jaw tight. Her eyes slid off of him easily, and she turned from them all and passed back into the club room.

She heard them follow, polished shoes cushioned by a plush rug, bought from Irula's markets in the far west but made by Novuran hands up in the scattered mountain villages. They'd lost their berths in Irula two years ago. There would be no more fine rugs, not of this pattern, not of this make.

They were losing so much, but now that the burning ship was out of sight, the men arranged themselves about the room, fashionably at ease. Evelyn took up her customary position across from the sideboard, by the windows, where she would be forgotten for as long as she remained silent, and set apart when she did not. Mr. Urston, owner of the plagued clipper, still looked pinched and thin; he alone remained near her, gazing at the dark blankness of the glass.

"The only good thing to come out of all of this," Mr. Sing said, pouring himself and Urston a brandy, "is that there are no more tariffs."

There were no more tariffs because there would soon be no more money at all. Ship trade was the only thing keeping the wheezing lungs of Delphinium's finances breathing. The workshops were running low in raw materials and far-flung customers, the warehouses only receiving in new goods once every few weeks.

And yet it was enough for the next week, the next month, the next year if they were lucky; they would continue on pretending that everything would be fine. This group spoke around death, avoiding it assiduously. And so they would not see when at last it came for them.

She considered giving another easily-ignored warning, then

abandoned the notion and moved to the door. "Gentlemen," she said, softly. "I will see you next week."

She left to half-hearted acknowledgments, descending a finely-hewn set of stairs nestled along the side of the restaurant that the club office sat atop of. Even six months ago, she would have heard the soft roar of conversation through the wooden paneling, but tonight the restaurant was quiet. Not empty, not yet, but growing thin and patchwork.

The other merchant lords avoided death, but Evelyn knew its contours and its character intimately, marking its creeping progress day by day. It had been her sole companion since she was a girl of seven, her mother gasping for breath, scrabbling for her hand, dying. A few years later, she lost her father. Then her brothers. She lost her whole household, until she was the only one left standing before the edifice of her father's business, draped in her black veil and her high-necked mourning dress, alone and called to the seat of power. Death had borne her out of the quiet servitude of girls and into trade deals, warehouses, a web of connections and strength.

"Ma'am?" came a voice from the bottom landing of the steps.

Evelyn slowed her descent, fingers twisted in her heavy skirts. The boy who handled the coats was missing, replaced by a girl maybe sixteen years old, her face scarred on her left cheek with pockmarks. She looked healthy, though, round-hipped and broad-faced. She also looked terrified.

Ah. The supplicant.

It was rare that girls came to her from the working masses; this one was Violetta's doing. Evelyn descended the last few steps, coming abreast of the girl and peering into her eyes.

The girl recoiled. "I'm sorry, ma'am, I didn't mean—"

"You are certain this is what you want?" Evelyn asked.

The girl was shaking, hard enough that her shoulders moved, that her dark hair piled on top of her head shivered in the lamplight.

"I... that is..."

Evelyn gestured impatiently, and the girl handed over Evelyn's heavy, oil-coated cloak, and with it the small case Evelyn had brought with her. It wasn't a fashionable thing, but inside it was cunningly divided into a warren of small chambers. Evelyn opened the clasp and drew out the small vial containing the boiled pulp of white bryony root.

The girl stared at it.

Evelyn glanced up the staircase, but none of the men had yet emerged. They wouldn't, not for at least another hour. Her departure always had the same effect as the ladies of the house repairing to another room after a dinner party. The brandy would flow more heavily, the tobacco clouds grow larger overhead. They would tell themselves they deserved to relax, now that she was gone.

She didn't mind that part of it. Tobacco was a noxious weed.

Evelyn leaned in, pressing the vial into the girl's hand. "It will not be pleasant."

"Real plague isn't pleasant," the girl responded, voice wavering. "It will be convincing enough? They'll send me to one of the border hospitals?"

And from there to escape, no doubt. A bold plan, if a foolish one. She was just as likely to sicken for real inside those fetid buildings. "Take no more than two droplets every twelve hours, less if your body reacts strongly. You will need the rest periods. It will be very bitter, and is caustic to the skin, so make sure to take it with as much water as you can stand."

Evelyn waited for the girl to ask for more: more help, advice on how best to smuggle it into the hospital, on what to do if she took too much.

Instead, she reached for the small coin purse hidden in the folds of her skirt.

Evelyn stepped back. "No need," she said. "Just be gone from this place. You do this to yourself. I had no hand in it."

"Of course, ma'am." The girl curtsied. Evelyn closed up her case, drew her cloak over her shoulders, and stepped out of the building.

Her assistant, Violetta Fusain, waited in the high-wheeled carriage parked down at the corner. The footman opened up the carriage door for Evelyn, and provided the block to step up. She took her seat across from her white-clad attendant, so different from herself, but with no less quickness in her lowered eyes.

Violetta's pale hair was drawn back from her cherubic face. She looked like a delicate doll, except for the sharpness of her gaze.

The door shut behind her. "I have met with your girl," Evelyn said. "It is done. I have delivered her poison."

Violetta frowned at that. "Poison? She asked for medicine."

"A medicine that sickens is poison. And she will be lucky if she does not die from it, but she seemed determined."

Violetta grimaced, but did not argue. The carriage pulled out into the street, passing by the first turning towards home and instead rattling down the hillside, toward the harbor below.

Something had happened, then.

"*The Verity?*"

"Has encountered a problem, my lady."

"A plaguing problem?" She thought of burning masts, great beacons of blazing failure upon the water. She could afford to lose a ship, but not her reputation. But when she searched Violetta's face for pain or frustration, she found neither.

Instead, she found fear.

"No, my lady," Violetta said. "Something else entirely."

chapter two

The ship rolled gently below her feet, wood creaking on all sides. With the sun long set, there were no calling gulls to hear, and on the first night in dock, there were few sailors aboard. She was left with only the wash of the water and the drum of the rain that had started up halfway to the harbor.

"Should we call for a doctor, my lady?" the captain asked.

Evelyn looked down into the staring eyes of the first mate of *The Verity*. Behind her, Violetta lifted the small oil lantern she carried a few inches higher. The light danced across the man's pupils, but nothing in his face responded in the slightest. His eyes did not narrow, his jaw did not twitch.

And yet he breathed.

"How long has he been like this?" Evelyn asked, mind racing. She had heard of catatonias before, but none like this man's. There was no limb rigidity, no rictus grin; nor was there any torpor, no deep and unceasing slumber. It was as if the soul of him had simply winked out, leaving an otherwise normal husk of a man who breathed, whose heart beat, but who could not move.

A fly landed on the man's iris. He did not blink.

"Barely an hour, my lady," said Luc Reynolds, her ship's captain. "I was with him at the pub when it came over him."

"How many others?"

He hesitated, then said, "Five, my lady. That we know of. Not everybody has been located yet, not the men who went home to their families or other embraces. If you understand me."

"I understand you, Captain," she said, looking away from the living corpse at last. Reynolds had his hat in his hand, and he looked scared.

She had never seen him look scared before.

"The others are in the brig. Shall I fetch a doctor, my lady?"

"Not yet," she said. "Find everybody. Find anybody else in this state. If I am going to tell the magistrates that my ship has brought an unknown illness onto Delphinium's soil, then I will have it quarantined before I do so." Internally, she was cursing, pacing furiously, rending her hair. Outwardly, she was almost as still as the sailor beside her.

"Of course, my lady," Reynolds said, glancing between her and Violetta. "I…suppose it's best to tell you now, that before I met him at the pub, he went I don't know where."

Worse and worse. The unknown number in whorehouses now were bad enough. "And the other five?"

"The same. They scattered to the winds."

It was almost normal, almost expected, but the timing was off. For the first mate and the others to have gone to their business and come back to the pub so quickly, they must have left immediately after the crews began unloading cargo. The other five sailors had shirked work, and the first mate had barely been better. Understandable, except that meant they abandoned their brothers, the men they had sailed with for months. More than that, it had meant risking the loss of drink, paid for by the officers. It wasn't like them.

The look upon Captain Reynold's face said that he agreed with her.

"Something rotten," he offered, softly. "It looks like witchcraft."

Evelyn lifted one pale hand, waving off the suggestion. The last witches had been tried centuries ago, and it was her understanding that the Judiciary would have preferred the entire subject disappear into obscurity, a dark blot on their history. After all, the witches slaughtered had been mostly women, mostly widows, mostly orphans. Women alone were always a threat, but to call it *magic* was…uncivilized.

Better to give them a quiet corner to call their own and move on. Delphinium had certainly benefited from doing as much for her.

"What should we do with him?"

Evelyn thought back to her pay ledgers. "He is unmarried."

"Yes, my lady."

"And the others?"

"Two are without a wife."

"Kill those two, along with him."

The captain went very still, and behind her, she heard Violetta gasp. Her fingers itched, the old scars tightening. She was no stranger to death, but perhaps one to ordering it. They certainly seemed to think it fit her ill.

"My lady—" Violetta began.

Evelyn turned and fixed her with a calm look. "We must assume this is some sort of plague. The three unmarried men have nobody to miss them, and so it makes the most sense to end their illness swiftly, to prevent its spread. The others… we may preserve them for the doctors, I suppose."

"I am not at sea," Reynolds said, finally finding his voice, his gaze fixed on her as if he could not bear to look at his first mate. "My authority doesn't extend this far. The Judiciary—"

"Killed fifty-seven men today aboard *Constance* because of plague. They will understand. The other three, keep them in the brig. Set a guard. Then go down the roster and locate every man who served aboard, and find out if we have lost them, as well. Once you have taken the measure of our problem, *then* you might call the doctors."

Reynolds worked his bristled jaw, searching for words, perhaps for courage. "I would prefer to lock them all up together, my lady. They are my men."

"I think you will find that they are mine." She looked at the unfortunate soul. He had been a worthwhile investment, until now. Certain acts of fortune could not be prepared for. *Constance* had been an excellent demonstration of that.

But…if she pushed now, Reynolds might leave her for Danforth or Sing's ships, perhaps without carrying out her orders at all. And if the sickness could spread from man to man, the whole ship needed to be put down, and disposing of the three men who didn't possess a family to complain to her wouldn't help them at all.

"I defer to your experience," she said at last, meeting Reynolds' gaze as he sagged in relief. He likely couldn't see her face, save for the pale tip of her nose pressed to the gauze of her veil. It meant he couldn't see her frustration, either. "Hold them as you will, and send me a report in the morning of what you and the doctors find."

"Yes, my lady."

Evelyn took one last look at the unmoving man, the fly still perched upon one round, now-dry sclera. And then she turned and climbed up out of the bowels of the ship, onto the rainswept boards. A small roof shielded her while, at her heels, Violetta set down her lantern to open up her umbrella.

"A lucky thing," Violetta said, "that the storm held off until *The Verity* was docked and unloaded."

Evelyn's lips quirked. Violetta's sense of humor was better formed than hers, but still a pale and twisted thing. A lucky thing indeed.

Once Violetta had everything in hand once more, they left the ship behind. Evelyn tallied the survivorship fees she would need to pay out to the three married men's spouses, and returned to the matter of when and how to involve the Judiciary. It was clear now that she had little chance of containing the situation before delivering it to them, neatly wrapped; without Captain Reynolds' dedicated aid, she didn't have the resources. So she worked through a list of the maritime judicial officers who might still be at their posts that night and would be sympathetic. The burning of *Constance* likely meant that at least a few of the diurnal regulars had stayed on, but the growing squall would have hurried most of those home again. The furrowed streets could drain off most of the flooding, but the cobbles would still be slick and dangerous in the darkness.

As they reached the end of the pier, Evelyn spotted a familiar figure in the gloom, standing beneath his own umbrella, illuminated by a street lamp that had not yet guttered out. He was speaking with a man Evelyn recognized as one of Urston's managers, who had no umbrella and was clearly eager to move on. Violetta had proven correct. The burning of *Constance* and the turn of the weather were both good luck for her; of all the men of the Judiciary who stuck their noses into her affairs, he was the least bothersome.

She approached Officer Linden Pollard directly and reached him just as Urston's man was hurrying back towards the main road. The roar of the rain drowned out her footsteps, but Pollard must have felt her approach, for he turned around to face her just as she came to a stop. Violetta beside her seemed to glow in the darkness, her pale dress reflecting back the lamplight onto the two of them in their dark clothing.

"Lady Perdanu," he said, inclining his head and carefully tipping back his umbrella so that he did not sheet water onto her. "What an odd time of night for you to be about. I hope you haven't had trouble with *The Verity*? My second said that her unloading proceeded very well this afternoon."

He had a smooth voice and smooth skin, marred only faintly by the furrows of age. His russet hair was mostly covered by his hat, and his high collar was still starched and bright white, despite the weather. On their first meeting, she had realized with disgust that he was handsome, but their subsequent meetings had proven that he had been able to rise above it.

"Officer Pollard. I do have a matter for your attention, unfortunately."

His soft smile faded in an instant, replaced with blank firmness. She appreciated it, as always. "Theft?"

"Worse." She nodded her head back towards the pier, to *The Verity*. "Six of my crew members have been captured by an illness."

"Like *Constance*'s crew?"

"No." That had been a coughing, retching plague, from what Violetta had reported and Urston later confirmed. "This is a far stranger illness. It's as if they are…empty."

"Empty?"

"Perhaps," she said, choosing her words with care, "it is a problem not only for the doctors, but for your men as well."

"You suspect poison."

Ah, but he was quick. She did appreciate him. "Or something like it. They don't appear ill at all, except that they don't move. They don't blink. They are empty."

"You think it might be the next move in the coup?"

She wanted to tell him that it was something she had never seen herself, but doing so would show too much of a hand she preferred to play only with serving girls and indelicate debutantes. To Linden, she would always be the strange heir to Perdanu Shipping Incorporated. What grew in her garden was a private matter.

"I think that it is strange, and that the timing is worrying. Nobody took ill until *after* they arrived."

He considered this, no doubt evaluating her words for likely honesty. Would it be a safer thing, for this to have been caused by poison in a home port? She wasn't sure.

"Well," he said, finally, "we may at least hope, then, that it hasn't spread far. I will look into the matter. May I offer my assistance in tracking down your wayward sailors?"

It would upset Reynolds, but it was better than letting her captain's tender feelings hide the other afflicted, now that he knew she meant to slaughter them. "Yes, if you would be so kind."

"Of course, my lady." He bowed to her, hand against his heart, umbrella once again tipped back to spare her. "Call on me tomorrow, that I might update you?"

She shook her head. "I make it a point not to come into town so often." She touched the hem of her veil with one hand, and he eased back a half-step, shifting his weight to his heel. Nobody mistook her for a delicate, damaged flower, but few doubted that such horrid grief could leave a woman untouched. Her veil was armor. Her veil was indispensable. "Send a letter, separate from my captain's updates. I would appreciate the added perspective."

"You don't suspect that he…?"

"No," she said. "But I do know that they are his men."

She left the rest unspoken, and after courteous goodbyes, Evelyn made her way back to her carriage. Violetta followed, a silent ghost at her side, half-sodden where the umbrella hadn't covered her.

chapter three

"Have you ever seen its like before?" Violetta asked, pitching her voice to be heard above the rain pounding on the carriage roof. Their driver took them slowly up into the towering hills that surrounded the bowl of Delphinium. Combined with the drainage of the River Larkspur and the sea itself, those hills damned the poorer citizens below to a life on the verge of submersion, but scaling them held other dangers. The cobbling had only recently been extended to all the great houses, and the sides of the roads still gave way occasionally, loosing stones or slicking them with silt and mud. Their driver took his time, especially with the clouded, starless sky above.

"No," Evelyn said. "I know of nothing that could provoke that response, in animal or man."

Violetta grimaced. She had no doubt been hoping that Evelyn would know an antidote. The girl, barely twenty-five, sometimes had a faith in Evelyn that bordered on the ridiculous.

When Violetta looked at her, she saw…what? A lonely woman, doing her best with the hand that had been dealt to her? Or did she somehow see the tremor in Evelyn's scarred hands, the pinched thinness of her face, the rot staring out from behind her eyes, and still not care?

She couldn't.

The carriage rattled to a stop. Above the din of the rain, Evelyn thought she heard a shout. Then the carriage bobbed; the driver had dismounted.

Violetta leaned forward and peered through the window in the door. "I can't see him, my lady. Should I—?" She hesitated, no doubt because the heavy layers of fabric she wore were still soaked through where Evelyn's umbrella had not protected her. The hair on the drenched side of her head was threatening to come down from its pins, drying slowly against her cheek.

Evelyn arched a brow. Violetta huffed a resigned laugh, then opened the door out into the squall. She stepped out, then looked back. Evelyn held up a hand: leave the door open.

Violetta nodded, then struck out along the road, disappearing into the darkness. She had left the lantern with Evelyn, who moved it to the far side of the carriage and lowered its shade, allowing her eyes to adjust to the darkness outside. She could see Violetta moving, pale and reflective against the black. She watched her pick her way along the road, and then off of it, steps turning sucking and heavy. And then she knelt.

Something was there, at the side of the road.

The rain refused to gentle as Violetta stood back up, turning towards the carriage. Whatever it was, if it had once lived, it was surely drowned now. Evelyn eased herself back into her seat and turned the lantern back to full glare as Violetta regained the road and came to the door.

"It's a man," Violetta said. "He's still breathing."

Not drowned at all. "A drunk?"

"No, my lady. We think he's injured."

"And what does he think?"

"He's unconscious. Breathing, but not well."

Of course.

The options that lay before her were all unappetizing. To leave him would invite the disgust of her servants, and it had taken her years to find Violetta and even a driver who did not mind going into and out of the city in such rains, in such darkness. To take him back down to the closest hospital would add another hour to their journey, and the weather would only worsen.

And she did not want a convalescing house guest.

But the last option was the simplest. "Bring him here, then. He can sleep off whatever ails him at the manor."

Violetta looked relieved as she ducked back out of the carriage.

It took them another ten minutes to get the man over to the road and hoisted into the seat across from Evelyn. Violetta settled in beside her, hair fallen down from her pins and clothing turned grey and muddy. The carriage lurched back into motion, and Evelyn lifted the lantern to get a better look at her new guest.

He was just on the cusp of middle age, at most only a few years older than herself, with high cheekbones and a broad jaw that unbalanced his visage. Or, perhaps, the blame could be laid at the contusions that puttied his face, the blood dried on his cracked lips. He had been severely beaten, and Evelyn suspected that beneath his clothing he had broken ribs, or worse.

Somebody had wanted him dead. Somebody...

Somebody had seen the tattoo that peeked out beneath his workman's shirt collar. Evelyn reached forward and pulled the fabric back just a few inches, exposing black ink mapping out the pattern of an Imperial soldier. An officer, given that it encroached on his neck.

Her heart sped up.

"My lady," Violetta said, voice low. "He's..."

A traitor. Did that still scan? How could he have betrayed the country, if his fellows *ruled* that country? But the Judiciary served the empire, and in the eyes of Delphinium, this was still a war. This was still a rebellion.

"We need to report him," Violetta said.

Report him, and draw the Judiciary's attention. Even if the situation with *The Verity* blew over quickly, the increased scrutiny would be unwelcome. *Kill him*, whispered the part of her that had been so quick to the slaughter in the harbor. Easier, surely, and easily done with him already unconscious, and the rain so fierce.

They could leave the body by the side of the road. Farther out, into the fields. Violetta would do it, given the fear now on her face.

But no; there were other uses for a soldier, a traitor, a man so covered with ink that it spoke to high rank. She had known it from the moment she saw those tattoos. Her heart was a pounding drum inside her chest.

Evelyn considered her assistant for a moment, then said, "He stays in the house."

Violetta flinched, shocked. "He—he will be a problem."

"Have you ever known me to not act in the defense of my home?" That cowed her quickly, and Evelyn's features softened. She looked back at the soldier, imagining the wealth of information he must possess. "He stays in the house, and we keep him cloistered. He will know much that can be of use. Movements at the borders, perhaps the structure of the blockades. He may even know what manner of plague has struck our sailors."

Violetta shifted, uneasy and afraid. "The Judiciary can learn as much from him. It is not our responsibility. My lady, to even have him in this carriage puts us in danger if we don't report him. Puts *you* in danger."

It did. If the Judiciary found them out, they could have her hanged for treason. A good citizen did not obscure contact with the enemy. It was not a risk she would have taken a year ago. But now, with Delphinium rotting beneath her, Evelyn looked on the bloodied body across from her and saw only opportunity. "If we find him out, we gain the upper hand. We help the city, and strengthen our own position."

"And if he is no defector? If he will not tell us what he knows, if he tries to harm us?"

"Then we will break him."

chapter four

Evelyn hid the soldier in one of the unused bedrooms in the manor's inner sanctum, a set of rooms that she kept to almost exclusively and that let out upon the greenhouse. Only Violetta and two maids Violetta had personally selected were allowed in those halls, a modicum of privacy that Evelyn clung to even as she needed people to change her sheets, to cook her food. It was useful now apart from her more personal paranoid fancies; it meant that they could ensure only she and Violetta tended to the sickroom and saw their patient's tattoos.

She left Violetta to clean him up and moved deeper into the house, lantern swaying in her hand. Close to the door to her gardens, she kept a small workroom, locked by a single key she kept on her person at all times. She opened the door and slipped inside, setting the lantern on a hook.

Evelyn looked over the array of unlabeled jars and boxes that she had accumulated over the years, organized according to a specific pattern held only in her mind. Goldenrod to slow bleeding, willow bark to dull the pain, ginger to push off infection. She was no doctor, but she was skilled enough to nurse a man back to health.

Or put a man in the ground.

Poisons lined her shelves, white bryony and belladonna, oleander and aconite. Some a magistrate would recognize by name, but many were more esoteric, like the bottle of gelsemium tincture, its stopper crusted over in the decade since she'd used it last. She'd tended the plant, harvested the root, powdered it and infused it into clear grain alcohol obtained from a chemist ostensibly for the extension of an old bottle of perfume from her childhood. Mixed into a glass of spirits, the clear poison was all but tasteless and took hours to strike. Two, four, as many as eight hours after ingestion, breathing would become difficult, the lungs begin to slow and fail. The body would become cold, the heartbeat rapid and feeble. Eventually, inevitably, death would follow.

Gelsemium killed without pageantry. There was only a quiet death in the middle of the night, and in the morning, a body born out of the house to the tower mausoleums, built above ground so that the drowning floods could not reach the bodies inside.

Her father had been first.

He had made plans to marry her off to Lord Susthin, knowing of his pox, knowing of his clenched fist, of the servants in his household that he had hurt, and of his first wife who had died of a miscarriage occasioned, it was whispered, by violence, and not ill-luck. Her father had been less quick to the strap than Susthin, but they had been of a kind, and Evelyn had always been only a nuisance, a daughter who could accomplish nothing. Even if her mother's young death had not devastated her soul, Evelyn would never have been a beauty, and the grief that clung to her from age seven had drawn her thin and translucent. It made her reserved, unpredictable, and angry.

Evelyn had been so *angry*.

And so she had decided she would not submit. She made a gelsemium tincture and slipped it into his brandy. He had been dead before dawn.

Nobody suspected her. Nobody questioned her obvious grief. If suspicion fell, it fell on her brothers alone, who stood to gain the whole of the fortune and the shipping company. And back then, before the coup, Perdanu Shipping had been wealthy beyond imagining. They did not possess much political influence, due to the relative youth of their title, but it would come in time, and silks and spices and gold went a long way to securing power. But if suspicion fell, she never heard about it at all.

Her brothers shut her away, claiming that her grief was so acute she must rest. She had accepted it, until she tried the door from her chambers and found it guarded by servants who, apologetic and false-tongued, would not let her leave. The marriage was not called off. Lord Susthin visited her, and though he kept his hands to himself in deference to her black veil, she could feel his disdain, his repulsion. He didn't want her. He wanted her money.

So did her brothers. She could hear them talking, sometimes, late at night as they prowled the halls, arguing and drunk, about how best to make money off of her, how best to forge alliances. Should they break the engagement her father had designed, and try someone another step up the rungs of power? No, better to get her away from them, worthless creature that she was. She had always been the weak one, the fragile one.

And so everybody mourned for her when her brothers died not a fortnight later. They mourned for the constant tragedy of her life, and they mourned for a girl left alone, so unsuited to isolation, so unsuited for the fortune that had been dumped into her lap as the bodies dropped around her.

None of them had ever suspected.

They were all fools.

Poison was not the only tool she had. Behind the bottles she kept certain papers, secrets and promises stored for when she had need. Violetta would surely prefer to see their soldier buried in the garden, no risk at all, and Evelyn couldn't blame her; they could both feel the vultures circling. If the Judiciary learned of this, if Danforth and Sing and the others knew, they would come for her. They would strip her of her wealth, of her safety. She was one of the last full-bodied beasts left in their ever-tightening prison, and the jackals would tear her apart if they saw weakness, if only to buy themselves a few more years.

But as long as the soldier remained hers, she had power. He had become her secret the moment he had stepped across the border, set on whatever path would bring him so near to her doorstep. He couldn't have chosen to escape to a dying city. He wouldn't have chosen the winding road that led to her home at random.

In some way, he was here for *her.*

And so she would nurse him back to health. She would spool out his secrets from him and see what she could gain. It was a risky move, but she had not gotten to where she was by being meek, only paranoid. Only proud.

The vultures circled, regardless of what she did, how still she kept, how small she made herself. No; her secret soldier would give her the upper hand.

But she did not have to grant him power over her in exchange. She looked over the rows of medicines and poisons, considering. Datura, to make him delirious, to keep him from ever learning anything about her that he could twist to hurt her? No; she needed him coherent, able to answer questions. Incapacitation could come later, if he healed enough to attempt escape. For now, what she needed was a way to keep her identity hidden in case he did one day fall into the hands of the authorities. She took down several jars from the shelf and worked quickly, powdering a dried, gnarled root and mixing it with steeped liquids. She made just enough to fill a small vial, and tucked it into her case along with the medicines she had already gathered.

By the time she returned to the sickroom, Violetta had left. The soldier had been stripped to the waist, his torso bruised and bloody over the thick black tattoos that had been worked into his flesh from hip to shoulder, and halfway down his arms. An officer for sure. The tradition had started over a hundred years ago, a point of pride among the men the empire sent halfway around the world to fight for it. A young soldier had the head of a leviathan poked in ink into the flesh between his shoulder blades, and it grew from there in a language that spread from ship to ship. The higher a soldier rose, the more skin his tattoos covered. The generals and admirals had black ink curling along their hairline, though the reigning empire had called it a monstrous tradition. It should have been the first clue that a schism was coming.

Evelyn sat, gingerly, on the edge of the mattress. She set out the contents of her case. Poultices to cleanse the skin and speed healing. The clotting agent, the pain killer.

But first…

She drew a pipette of tincture of belladonna, blended with powdered root of black hellebore, and leaned in close. The soldier moaned but did not stir as she eased apart his eyelids. His eye was unfocused, the sclera tinged red by burst blood vessels. She carefully applied three drops to his pupil, and watched as it grew in size, a deep blackness in the room's dim light. Then she let his eyelids fall shut and moved to the other side of his face, repeating the procedure.

He only whimpered in his unconsciousness as the tincture burned out his eyes.

chapter five

The soldier slept for the next two days, Evelyn's medicines keeping him in a sedated fog. Violetta was left to clean his bedding when he evacuated himself, and the bedroom's lack of windows trapped the stench, turning Evelyn's stomach on her visits. But the swelling began to lower, the bruises turning sickly yellow instead of brilliant, deep maroon. In another day, she could ease him back to wakefulness, to blindness, to her questions.

For now, though, her attention was focused on the letters stacked on her work desk, the ledgers open to her left. She had men to do her accounting for her, and she employed them, but she kept a private record of her sales, her holdings, her wealth. Her power. Her ledgers were expanding by fewer and fewer lines each month, and her power would begin to fade soon, without the endless growth to sustain it.

The boundaries of her world were drawing inward. The noose was tightening.

The letters ranged from invitations to dinners she would never attend to requests from merchants who were trying to jump past the men she had hired to interact with them. Most would be burned. There were, however, three letters she would attend to: from Captain Reynolds, from the doctors, and from Officer Pollard.

They all reported much the same thing. After every crew member had been accounted for, seven in total remained in a catatonic state. The doctors had been unable to find a cause. The wives of two had requested a merciful death for them (and Reynolds informed her of the death payments he would be making to the widows). The rest had been moved to one of the sanitariums outside the city limits.

Perhaps the same one Violetta's girl had been trying to get to?

Evelyn massaged her temple, fingers slipping up beneath the short veil she wore in her home. It came down only to the tip of her nose, allowing her to eat and drink on the rare occasion she remembered to. She still wore her stiff-necked mourning dress, but that was only for the benefit of the servants. Half her grief was an affectation, a shield. Only the smallest bit of veil served to mark her actual loss.

The period of mourning for her mother had passed twenty years ago, but Evelyn would not forget her so neatly. She owed her better than that.

Pollard's letter, she was frustrated to find, requested that she return to the dock offices to fill out some paperwork related to clearing *The Verity* for continued travel into and out of the city. He could have sent it directly to her, for her to complete and return. Why summon her? She pressed her fingers a little harder into her skin, twisting her nails into her thinning auburn hair. Perhaps he wanted to question her. Perhaps her ship would not be cleared at all, and he wanted to discuss it with her in person.

There were no good reasons for him to summon her. That much was certain.

She continued with her morning tasks, and checked on her patient one last time, before she called for Violetta to ready their carriage. The rains cleared as she waited, sitting still and quiet in the foremost parlor, gazing out at the hill on which her house rested.

At last, Violetta came in to fetch her, and they climbed

together into the carriage and set off down to Delphinium.

The cab smelled not at all of the rescued soldier, his blood and filth scrubbed off the seat that Violetta now sat on. Its absence served as its own reminder. There were no traces left of him beyond the interior chambers of the mansion, just as she had requested.

But the coachman knew. Was it Evelyn's imagination, or had he been slow to shut the carriage door, hoping for some explanation, uncertain at what he'd been drawn into? And what of the servants, preparing food for an unseen guest? Violetta was the only one to tend to him directly, but she could not make broth for him without the cook knowing.

They would talk, and Violetta could only do so much to quiet them.

As Evelyn turned her options over, the carriage wound its way down from the hills, water rushing beside them in the deep gutters. The cobbles remained slick, but with full sunlight her driver managed to make good time. As houses and businesses began to grow in density, Violetta leaned into the central space, looking out the window in the door.

It was the same path they always took. There was nothing of interest out that door.

Violetta's brows drew together in confusion, before she surged up out of her seat and banged on the roof of the carriage for their driver to stop. She pressed herself against the door, face against the small window.

"What is it? Another discarded soldier?" Evelyn asked, biting back harsher words. The sooner she reached Pollard's offices, the sooner she could be back in her home, guarding her prisoner.

"No, my lady. It's—what is she *doing*?"

Evelyn frowned, leaning towards the door herself. A light touch at her shoulder moved Violetta enough out of the way that Evelyn could look out as well.

And there, standing in the muck by the side of the road, was the girl she'd given the bryony to at the club. Her hair hung limp around her face, unwashed and unstyled, and her clothing sat strangely, as if she'd forgotten how to dress herself. But where Evelyn would have expected her expression to match the pitiful state of the rest of her, she found the girl's eyes alive and bright. She was focused wholly on the carriage door, and a small smile played upon her lips.

She took a step towards the carriage, then another, reaching the cobbles and then crossing the drainage channel.

She did not blink.

"It's not natural," Violetta breathed, and reached up to bang on the carriage roof again. Evelyn reached out and caught her wrist.

"No," Evelyn said.

"The remedy you gave her—"

"Bryony does not do this," Evelyn said.

"She doesn't look right, my lady. We should go." Violetta pulled against Evelyn's grip, but Evelyn did not relent.

"Something in her eyes," Evelyn murmured. "There's something in her eyes." The girl was only a few feet away now, and her face lit with an unearthly delight as Evelyn pushed Violetta out of the way, coming into full view through the window.

"Evelyn Perdanu," the girl said. Her muffled voice had a strange tremor to it, a warbling that made Evelyn's spine stiffen, made her hands feel unaccountably cold. The horses were whickering, and the carriage rocked as they shied from the girl. They could sense it, the strangeness that Evelyn could see in every ill-animated line of her face. And those eyes, those unblinking eyes—

A fly landed on the girl's eye, and none of her features so much as twitched.

"The ship," Evelyn breathed. "Just like the ship."

"But better than the ship," the girl said, as if she could hear Evelyn through the door. Her smile widened. "We will not go out with the tide, now."

She came another step closer, and the horses revolted. The carriage threatened to overturn, to jerk forward, to be pushed back.

And then her driver came down from the box, brandishing his whip. The girl did not turn to him, ignored his shouts to get off the road. The whip fell once, twice upon her upper back, too lightly to cause serious injury. But the girl fell, all the same, suddenly an empty, motionless doll, dress and hair spilling into the gutter.

Her eyes remained open. Her face became slack. A thin line of blood trickled across her temple.

The driver looked to Evelyn, face stricken.

She eased open the door with shaking hands, stepping down from the carriage, heavy black skirts trailing behind her. She went to the girl, crouching down and reaching for her throat. She half expected the girl to grin again, to leap up, but she was as still as *The Verity*'s first mate. Her pulse was tangible, though uneven. Blood was beginning to spread out from where her skull had struck the cobbles.

"I didn't—" the driver began, then stopped. "I wasn't—"

"She is ill," Evelyn said. She had no room in her for her employee's shame; there was only stunned silence, growing fear. "She fell counter to your blows. It was not your hand that did this."

But better than the ship, she'd said *Better than the ship*. Moving, yet still catatonic. The mad light in her eyes had been only the animate version of her now-unblinking stare. They were linked. It was spreading.

It was spreading, and it had arrived on her ship.

"What do we do?" Violetta asked. She was hanging back, trembling. "We cannot bring her in the carriage, not if she is ill. And we cannot leave her here."

Kill her, burn her, bury her. She did not want to deal with this. She wanted it to be gone.

Evelyn watched as the girl's lips began to pale. Her breathing was growing shallower. The blow to the back of her head, combined with the dull state the sickness left her in, were working together swiftly. "We will not have to do either," Evelyn said. "She is all but dead. We will alert the Judiciary and have them send somebody out to handle the body."

Violetta swallowed. "But to leave her here—"

"If we took her, she would still die. But if it pleases you, we can remain by her side until she breathes her last." She looked between Violetta and the shame-faced driver.

Neither said a word.

Evelyn turned back to the girl. She didn't struggle or look like she was dying. As long as Evelyn didn't look into her eyes, she didn't look unnatural, just pathetic. Evelyn clung to the image. Perhaps she had been wrong. Perhaps she was only over-sensitive.

Another few breaths. And then—nothing.

"There," Evelyn said. "Now, may we continue upon the road?"

Violetta returned wordlessly to the carriage. The driver went to tend to the horses, who had become calm once more.

chapter six

We will not go out with the tide, now.

The girl's face clung to her thoughts as she sat through an awkward exchange with Officer Pollard's secretary, who informed her that he had been called away on some business but she was welcome to return the next day. It festered, haunting her on the return trip up the hills. It followed her into the depths of her house, into the sickroom of the soldier where he lay insensate, his promise bound up in danger. And it chased her into her workroom, where she shut herself into the close, green-smelling darkness and tried to breathe.

Sickness provoked delirium. Certain drugs, too. Perhaps—oh, but perhaps the catatonia was the result of a new compound, something her sailors had brought home with them, had distributed to a pretty girl met in a tavern, celebrating one last time before she risked her life to reunite with her family. Evelyn could picture it now. The sticky pulp of a flowering plant, rolled into a ball, chewed between the teeth, causing confused ecstasy. The affected, wandering and raving, delighted by the smallest thing and spouting out nonsense, until the pulp curdled in their bellies and suddenly twisted the effect. The delight turning to blankness, permanently or not.

That had to be it. And if the girl had met one of her sailors over a mug of ale, it made sense that she would speak in maritime-inflected riddles. That she might know Evelyn's name. There was no larger secret to it. None at all. And only coincidence had drawn the girl towards Evelyn's home, following the path of a disguised soldier.

And yet. And yet.

Something felt wrong.

The memory drew her in again: the cold upon her hands, the tension in her spine. She could hear the horses crying, see the fly moving across the girl's eye. If it had been a drug, wouldn't some of the men have partaken before they left the port they obtained it at? Wouldn't somebody have fallen into that stupor long before *The Verity* made dock?

Wouldn't the doctors have solved the puzzle?

No matter the cause, it was spreading. It was spreading, and her ship had brought it to Delphinium. She could feel the world pitch beneath her, threatening to shake her loose. If it continued to spread, would she be blamed? Would they burn her ships, take her power from her, drag her out before the magistrates? Search her home, find her poisons and her poultices and her traitorous captive? Her hands shook, her breathing coming in rapid, ragged bursts. She turned to the rows of bottles and began to fumble through them, the lantern she'd hung by the door casting barely enough light to work by.

She needed to be numb. She couldn't be afraid.

Evelyn pulled bottles by long practice, small vials of tinctures and large ceramic jars filled with dried rootstock. Her hands shook as she peeled, grated, pounded in mortar and pestle. She could have used alcohol, but it had never given her the particular kind of remove she craved. It didn't give her the ecstasy, the agony, the warping of the edges of the world until she was truly, perfectly alone, safe and floating in the void of her body, uncaring of everything around her. And while poppy juice might bring her close to what felt like death, she would be too insensate to realize its closeness before she slipped over the edge. No, she crafted her own obliteration.

From her lantern, she lit a long match, and with that the burner below the alembic filled halfway with water. The rest of the ingredients needed to be boiled, in sequence, and she fed them into the glass neck, piece by piece. Acrid steam curled up around her, and she inhaled, deeply, holding the fumes in her chest. They burned her, making her head swim. Her mind began to dull.

No; she had to focus, make the finished draught.

At first, the work produced a blissful stillness in her, an absence of everything beyond the glass in front of her. She became focused and clear. But then her thoughts crept back in, sickly and pale, self-aware and sharp along the edges. *Broken, broken*, they whispered as she blew out the flame, took up the glass with tongs and swirled it to cool the milky fluid inside. When the glass was cool enough to touch, she poured it into the mortar, stirred it three times, and then lifted the bowl to her lips.

As she took the draught, her lips twisted with the sick, bitter pleasure of it. Giving in—it always felt like giving in. Giving up, in the most precious way she could. She might be killing herself, but she did so slowly and by her own rules. Her self-destruction was modulated. It was therapeutic. Let her kill herself as she chose to, for nobody else should have the pleasure.

She had earned this pain. She had earned this oblivion.

She sank to the floor, drawing her knees up to her chest. Her corset protested the curling of her spine, and she reached back, fumbling for the tiny buttons along her dress. She needed Violetta there, to undress her, to crack open her armor. But no; Violetta could never see her like this, could never see her weak and writhing, wretched and retching.

She should have demanded privacy before retreating into her workroom, sent Violetta away from the sanctum on some task. She had forgotten, in her panic. Where was her assistant now? And did she feel as sick as Evelyn did, as haunted by the fevered gaze of that girl?

Slowly, Evelyn pushed herself up to her feet. She almost fell over the hem of her skirts, lurching forward and catching herself against one of the shelves that lined the wall opposite her workbench. The lamp had guttered out, or perhaps her pupils were constricting, blinding her despite the light. She felt her way to the door, fumbled with the key, let herself fall out into the hallway. She pulled herself together again just long enough to lock the door and slip the key back onto her chatelaine. Around her, the walls of the house wavered, pulsed, shifted in texture.

The bedroom. The bedroom, or the garden. Those were her private places, her final sanctuaries. If she had been smarter, she would have taken the draught there, already comfortably ensconced in anonymity.

She was a few doors down from the sickroom, and she could hear the soldier's breathing, heavy and ragged, pulsing through the walls. She walked towards it, hand over hand along the rippling plaster, the colors of the paper bleeding onto her pale fingers in time with the movements of his lungs. He was so loud; was he dying?

The door opened up. Violetta emerged, beautiful Violetta, radiant in white, not afraid at all. Fear shook Evelyn's bones, shame curling around her heart. Against Evelyn's fingers, there was no change in the pulse of the walls. Against her ears, there was no change in the volume of the soldier's breathing, his lungs still shaking the foundations.

No. No, it was *her* breathing.

She laughed, helpless.

Violetta noticed her then, turning to stare wide-eyed at her, linens gathered in her arms. Soiled. Evelyn could smell it from here. Her stomach rebelled, softened and rotted from the fluid clotting in it. "My lady?"

Go away, go away. She needed to pull herself upright, force herself to be proper and in control. *Leave me be, I will see you in the morning.* But all Evelyn could see was the fear in Violetta's eyes. Violetta, in the carriage. Violetta, on the road. Violetta, reaching out to care for the refuse that was the soldier, fretting over the crumpled body of the addled girl.

Evelyn wanted that. She wanted to fall by the roadside, let Violetta take command of her fate.

Evelyn reached out for her.

Cursing under her breath, her voice so soft and delicate,

Violetta locked the sickroom door and dropped the linens, hurrying to her side. She smelled of the soldier, of the sickroom, of the medicines Evelyn had instructed her to give him whether he woke or dozed. She smelled of all that Evelyn had done, and Evelyn took her proffered arm, leaning in to inhale deeply.

"Should I call for the doctor, my lady?" Violetta murmured, leading her down the hallway. "Is this the sickness? The sickness from the road, from *The Verity*?"

Evelyn shook her head, tangling her fingers into the frills along the waist of Violetta's gown. "No," she replied, voice alien to her own ears. "No, just a bath. A bath, Violetta."

Violetta had come to her four years ago as a simple maid, but she had always been special. Delicate, yet decisive. Watchful, yet discrete. Evelyn had cleaved onto her, raised her salary, made her head of the household staff, because she had wanted somebody like Violetta all her life. She had found in her somebody she could trust to watch the maids that came and cleaned her bedchamber, so that she no longer had to do it.

Ah, but she needed Violetta. Longed for her approval. She should feel shame, only shame, for Violetta to see her weakness so clearly, and yet it was an easy thing to do now—wasn't it?—to ask for her gentle hands to pry her corset loose, to watch her heat a kettle of water in the fireplace, fill the basin, prepare soaps and sponge and towel. Easier than to think of the girl dying at the side of the road.

She lost her moorings as Violetta slowly removed the pins in her hair, as she cleaned her arms and legs and stomach with hot, perfumed water. She caught those moments only in glimpses, the rest of her world contorting, stretching, darkening. She saw the townhouse her father had tried to move her to just after her mother's death, trying to break her mourning. She wandered the halls of that narrow house, and then of her own, all of them shivering and insubstantial, made of clumping, clotting shadows. She was alone. She was alone, and that was all she needed.

Then, back into her body, clothed in a chemise and wrapped in a blanket, tucked into the plush chair by the window. Violetta had not removed her veil even when she plaited Evelyn's hair, and that gesture of understanding brought tears to Evelyn's eyes.

But nobody was there to see them. Violetta had left.

To resume the laundry, or to flee?

Her stomach twisted at the thought. She had assumed she had seen loyalty and care in Violetta's eyes, but she had been wrong, so wrong. Of course she had felt nothing but disgust. Evelyn fixed upon how stricken she had looked, the soiled linens clutched to her chest. Bile rose in her throat.

No, not just bile. Her gut was cramping, savagely, fiercely. Something was trying to claw its way out of her. Incorrect dosage, she thought, weakly.

She only barely got herself out of the chair and to the chamberpot in time not to foul herself.

More time. Hours lost, half-dreaming nightmares, leaned against the wall by the pot. Wracking shivers. Violent vomiting, sometimes with Violetta there to hold her, sometimes not. She brushed against the precipice, toeing her way along the crumbling edge, feeling her body waver and shudder. A healthy woman could withstand this, but her? Her, with her weak bones and weaker flesh? Twice, she felt herself come close to tipping over, and there was no exhilaration to it. No delight, no relief, no fervent knowledge that she was destroying herself because she was tired, so tired, of preserving herself.

But she did not think about the girl with staring eyes. She did not think about the first mate of *The Verity*, catatonic below decks. She did not think about the soldier, or her guilt, or her need for him to mean something. She was given that one small mercy.

At some point, Violetta guided her to the bed, tucked her beneath the sheets. She perched on the edge of the mattress, against the heavy damask curtains that sagged from the beams above the bed, and watched her.

Slowly, Evelyn's senses sharpened. Her eyes focused. She regained perspective: her, incapacitated, shaking and standing at the shores of death. Violetta, watching, fearing. Violetta was an intelligent woman, and a caring one; she would have called for a doctor despite Evelyn's pleas. He would be on his way, and he would smell it on her, the poison, the filth of her, so different from a natural illness.

"Send the doctor away," she hissed.

"There is no doctor, my lady," she said. "You told me not to call one. I listened."

"Good," Evelyn said, quickly, too quickly. She wanted to reach out, but was too weak to do so. She hadn't meant to make Violetta look at her with fear. This was all so far beyond her control, all of it slipping away from her. She shuddered.

"My lady?"

Evelyn looked away, flushing with shame. She reached for the lie, but there was none close to hand. No; trust was all she had left to her. She had always trusted Violetta. Why would this be different?

"I miscalculated," she said, throat thick. Her heart pounded in her ears.

Violetta didn't ask for details, though. She reached beyond the heavy curtains and poured a cup of cool water. "Did it affect you so much? The girl?"

She understood.

The realization made her bones and lungs burn. Violetta understood. There was no judgment in her voice, and Evelyn could hardly believe it. "Yes," she said, wonderingly, hesitantly. "The girl. The soldier. Everything." Slowly, Evelyn pushed herself up, sheets falling into her lap. Her ribs stood out against her chemise and the thin, sallow skin below, her chest where it was bare turned splotchy red as the poison was mellowed by her flesh. "*The Verity.*"

"We can be thankful, at least, that it wasn't burned," Violetta said, offering the cup.

Evelyn drained the water and returned the cup to Violetta. She reached up to adjust the pins holding her veil in place. They had pulled out or broken sections of her fine, brittle hair, and the gauze refused to hang straight before her eyes. "Perhaps it should be," she said as she worked, focusing on the pain against her scalp instead of the drums of panic beating inside her chest. She could see it, the tarred ropes catching fire, the flames spreading, eating up one of her remaining twenty ships. "Perhaps the whole fleet should be burned. Perhaps the harbor should be closed."

"My lady?"

She looked at Violetta. She was attentive, and in command of the worry that flashed behind her eyes. "Have you ever thought of fleeing? Like the girl?"

"Who hasn't?" Violetta responded, easily. "But I would not abandon you, my lady."

Another wave of guilt surged through her, then faded in relief. She was glad for that, glad that Violetta would not leave her, not even after seeing her weakness. She took a shaking breath. "I am afraid, Violetta. I am afraid of what comes next. Because whatever took that girl, it was not plague."

Violetta paled. "What else could it be, though?"

"More rot, come to the city," Evelyn said. "A new threat, come to destroy our sailors, our laborers, the last lifeblood that we have. Whatever it is, whatever its cause, I brought it here, and we will be punished for it. A burned ship may be the best fate we can hope for."

chapter seven

Linden Pollard was in his office the next day, and he presented her with paperwork that he could have sent by courier, just as Evelyn had expected. Still, she took up the offered quill and signed off. *The Verity* would be cleared, through a combination of his influence and the doctors' inability to find any trace of actual sickness. He had no questions for her, did not know to ask about the girl, and she was more than happy not to tell him.

Once the ink was dry, he escorted her from his office, asking her about her plans for the coming social season (she had none), and if she thought *Constance* was an isolated event. Should they expect more sickness, more interference from what he feared would be a tightening blockade, or was it just an unhappy accident?

A spike of paranoia pushed against her spine, but she ignored it. He didn't know; he spoke only of the obvious threats to the city. "They won't need to," Evelyn said. "They are learning politics. The price we get for our goods is dwindling, and the prices we pay for grain are rising. Slowly but inevitably, they are working to starve us. No bloodshed needed."

He inclined his head, as if considering. But Officer Pollard was clever, quick-minded, and he surely already understood the shape of things. He looked around the front receiving room, with its clerks bent to their work, quills scraping over paper, then extended his arm. "Will you walk with me, my lady?"

Ah. He *did* have a reason for summoning her down, then. She was still wrung out from the night before, but she could not beg off with a claim of faintness. For all her delicacy, Lady Evelyn Perdanu of Perdanu Shipping did not faint.

So she took his arm, fingers taut and still on the sleeve of his uniform. "A turn, perhaps."

They stepped out into the grey light of a morning under threat of rain. Violetta, waiting at the carriage, dropped a small curtsy as they went by. She made as if to follow, but Evelyn moved her free hand in a tiny flash of pale skin against her dark skirts, and the girl subsided.

"I must confess," he said, when they were two blocks away from the central docks office, heading up the slope into a fashionable stretch of shops, "I don't understand why they don't just take the city. The Judiciary can't fend them off, and by now we're a half-starved hart, unable to flee."

"They know," Evelyn said, peering up at him through her veil. "And they would prefer us to surrender."

"But *why?*"

"To humiliate us. To ensure we know our place, and our value to them."

"Which is?"

"The people are as nothing. By now, all the traitors want are the roads and buildings, half-flooded, and perhaps a few ships if they can convince a merchant lord or two to switch sides." The thought sickened in her belly, which still jerked and trembled within the confines of coutil and whalebone from the abuse of the night before.

Linden grimaced. "I'm surprised nobody has."

"Perhaps some have, in small ways."

Linden stopped. He turned towards her, frowning. "Do you know something, my lady?"

She tilted her chin up, returning his piercing look. His brow was tight, his eyes shining. For a moment, her hands grew cold—but then he blinked, licking at his lips, clenching his jaw. No, he wasn't touched. He was scared. He worried for his city, just as she did.

"Perhaps," she said, slowly. Her thoughts went to the soldier locked in her sickroom. There were signs that the men of her club had met with military men of their own, or had their seconds carry on arrangements when they were safe in foreign lands. The prices of goods were dwindling, but not for all of them equally. Evelyn considered giving Danforth's name to Pollard; she was fairly certain that his clerks could uncover some discrepancy in his books. He could be dragged before a tribunal. He'd be executed for treason while the Empress watched impassively from her high tower.

It would open a power vacuum, and in a healthier age she would have pursued it, profited from it. Now, though, it would only damage the failing city. It would fatten her coffers in the short term, but by next year, they would all be the poorer for it.

And that was assuming that nobody discovered her own damning houseguest.

No, she would not give his name. "I couldn't swear to anything specific. It just seems...unavoidable."

Pollard looked disappointed. Unsettled. He looked away from her and began walking again, and she accompanied him as if nothing had been said at all.

They passed shop after shop, all with doors open but emptier floors than last season. Instead, the streets teemed with citizens in fine clothing, blocking their ornamented carriages from rolling forward. The formerly well-to-do surrounded them, drained of cash but dedicated to being seen. It was tragic pageantry, and by Pollard's face, he felt the sting of it. Evelyn felt more a dull disgust.

At least her dress would never go out of style, and she would never be required to join the dance. But she felt eyes on her, eyes she recognized, that recognized her in turn. Her skin crawled. With Pollard at her side, she had no hope of passing, unremarked, back into her shadows, and as they crossed the street, the door opened on a nearby phaeton. From it emerged a woman a few years younger than she was, with her hair dyed fashionably scarlet. She descended on Evelyn and Pollard in a rustle of rich golden silks, her neckline cut almost so low as to be only appropriate for a ball. Countess Gentine Urvenon, niece to the Empress, dedicated socialite.

Come, no doubt, to ask about the invitation that Evelyn had discarded the previous morning. That invitation, like all the ones before it, meant only one thing: Urvenon had need of her medicines. It was the only reason the noblewomen of the city tolerated her dour presence at their glittering parties.

"Lady Perdanu, how good to see you out," Countess Urvenon said, curtsying slightly. She glanced between Evelyn and Pollard, her hunger for what Evelyn had to offer now eclipsed by having spotted Evelyn with male company. It would provide gossip for at least a night, maybe longer. "And may I know the name of your walking companion?"

It wouldn't be out of character for Evelyn to simply turn and walk away, but Pollard would have been scandalized. So she held out an open hand in welcome. "Officer Linden Pollard, this is Countess Gentine Urvenon."

"It is an honor," Pollard said, bowing. Urvenon's eyes lit up as she watched the pull of his finely starched uniform across his broad shoulders.

"My, an officer of the Judiciary!"

"We are discussing business, Countess," Evelyn said, hoping to cut the conversation short. Then again, perhaps it would be better to leave Pollard to her, to let them find folly with one another. Her eyes drifted to the shifting crowds moving around them, wishing she could fade into nothing.

"Of course, of course," Urvenon said, Evelyn hearing her as if through a tunnel. "I only wanted to ask if you had received my invitation. The last several must not have reached you, as I never heard a response."

Her jaw clenched. She would have to accede to this one. Her mourning remove could only cover so much of her misanthropy. "I did," she said, glancing at Urvenon and then away, across the crowds. "I would be honored to attend."

Urvenon smiled. "And will you be bringing a guest? Officer

Pollard would certainly be welcome."

Pollard said something in return, but Evelyn's gaze had fixed on Urvenon's maid, still waiting by her carriage.

Urvenon's maid, looking straight at her. Unblinking.

"Lady Perdanu?" Pollard asked, and Evelyn looked back at him and Urvenon, eyes wide, lips parted. Her chest shivered, her lungs refusing to work.

"I apologize," she managed. "I thought I recognized—somebody."

"Everybody does seem to be out today," Urvenon agreed, warmly. "I'll leave you to your socializing. But please, do consider bringing Officer Pollard."

Evelyn nodded. She watched as Urvenon went back to her carriage, back to the maid. She watched the maid blink, incline her head, act entirely normal. She never turned to look at Evelyn.

"My lady?" Pollard asked, touching her hand lightly.

She shook her head. "I apologize," she repeated, and they began to walk again. "If the party interests you, you are welcome to come."

"As your guest?"

She looked up at him, feeling blank and hollow. "You need not accompany me to be welcome, if that is what worries you. Attend if you wish; I'm sure you will find your name on the list now."

He colored, shook his head. "While the invitation is flattering, I fear those sorts of engagements are not for me. I take it they are not for you, either."

"Hardly. But they are a hazard of my position," she murmured, gaze once more roving over the crowd. Those *eyes*. She couldn't shake the image, the chill that had settled into her spine. Her fingers perched on Pollard's arm pressed harder into his uniform sleeve. She must have imagined that unnatural attention, casting the maid's face in the shape of the bryony girl at the side of the road. The maid was healthy. But the bryony girl, she had been so undeniably afflicted. They hadn't told the constable yesterday when directing him to the body, desperate to hide any connection between her and Evelyn's ships. The weight of that secret now pressed up in her throat like a wave of vomit.

"My lady, is something the matter? You've gone pale," Pollard said, voice soft.

She would burn for this, if he knew that it was spreading. But if it was spreading, he would learn from someone else soon enough.

"Have you heard," she ventured, "any updates from the sanitarium?"

He shook his head. "Not since yesterday. I've heard of no new cases among your men, either."

She didn't have to speak, didn't have to say a single thing. But she found herself looking out into the crowd again, hunting for that piercing gaze. Nobody looked at her. The streets were full only of the grey bustle of bodies.

"It may be spreading," she said, softly.

Pollard frowned, then drew her off the main thoroughfare and close up against the nearby shop. "The report from the sanitarium said they had determined further cases unlikely, as nobody else on the ship's roster was exhibiting symptoms. That's why I cleared *The Verity*. Have *you* received an update today?"

"Yesterday," she said. She took a deep breath, keeping her features even and bland. "Though not from any doctor. I saw a girl, by the side of the road. She had the same blank stare."

Evelyn could still see her, lying broken on the cobblestones.

"Where is she now?"

Dead.

"I don't know," Evelyn lied. "It was only for a moment, but it was unmistakable. I think…"

That it was unnatural. That it was not illness. That it—

"I think my men might have brought a new intoxicant back with them from some other port. Not so tempting as poppy juice, at least, or more of them might have succumbed to it, but something that may have been passed between hands in the alleyways after their arrival."

"Their strange dispersal right after *The Verity* docked."

She nodded. The explanation still sat ill in her mind, but she couldn't bring herself to voice her other theory. Even Violetta had rejected the thought that this could be something beyond the workings of man and earth, something apart from plague or vice. If even Violetta did not believe her, what chance did she have of Pollard listening?

No, the important thing was that he was prepared, if it began to spread. Even if that meant holding her responsible for it.

She lifted her chin, meeting his troubled gaze. "I hope that there is a limited supply, and that the knowledge of where to obtain it is lost with the minds of the afflicted," she said. "But if it is not…"

"Then I'll have my officers ready." He covered her hand with his own. Her skin burned at the contact, and she almost pulled away. "I will do my best to shield you," he added, quietly.

Her breath caught. Her stomach twisted.

She felt once again as if she were going to be sick.

All the little signs fell into place then, making sense of the whole. He had summoned her to him when he had no need to. He had walked with her in the fashionable part of town. He had asked if he could go *with* her to the dance, though she had interpreted it as asking if he was *required* to go with her.

He would do his best to shield her.

In an instant, her comfort around him evaporated, and her mind dashed in twenty different directions, frantic and fevered. She was stiff beside him, unable to control the horrified, frightened expression on her face. He didn't see it, eyes downcast, and in that moment she thought to flee. She wanted to be gone, wanted to be in her carriage, wanted to be in her garden.

She did not want this. But oh, she did not want to burn, either. She wanted his protection, and hated that she needed to rely on it.

"Thank you," she said at last. It came out thin. Hollow. But he smiled.

They walked another ten minutes, back around to her carriage. They parted ways. He clasped her hand perhaps too warmly, and she managed a brittle little nod in return.

She climbed into the cab and trembled the whole drive back to the mansion.

chapter eight

"Your patient is awake, my lady," Violetta said. "And growing lucid. Do you still wish to speak to him?"

Evelyn didn't look up, focused on the earth she was turning with her bare hands, loam pushing up beneath her nails. "Yes," she said. "But not immediately. Has he tried speaking with you?"

"On several occasions, only this last successfully."

"And has he been made a fool?" Either from his injuries or from her medicines.

"No. He didn't proclaim a name and rank, so he must remember that he is on unfriendly soil."

Would a defector hide that information? Would he be so slow to throw himself on the mercies of his rescuers? Surely he could tell his tattoos were bared to the open air. Surely he knew he was compromised.

If he was hiding his name, did that mean—

She forced the thought away and hollowed out a bowl in the soil, then gently lowered a yarrow splitting in and mounded the earth around it. The garden's soil drained well due to a complex system of channels cut into the floor below, leading to pipes that ran into the cellar, where the water could be collected and used again. It was a world apart from the mud pit that the grounds surrounding the mansion were. Things planted here in her greenhouse thrived year round, and she had cultivated over a hundred species, competing with each other for sunlight and for her attention, some native and some brought from far away.

The rain had been kind for the last few days, holding off and allowing her to spend her waking hours bathed in watery sunlight. She had ignored her letters and ledgers for vines and rootstock. Another draught of medicine hadn't been a real option, not with her stomach still sore and delicate, and working until her wrists and hands hurt was the only other way to keep her panic over Pollard and the bryony girl and the spiraling death of the empire at bay.

She felt almost steady, now. Almost normal. Almost under control.

But there was still the soldier. If he knew to blame his caretakers for his blindness, he hadn't yet been lucid enough to say anything about it. If Violetta knew to blame her for it, she had chosen not to say anything. Evelyn was thankful for the respite. She did not want to justify herself to anybody.

"Has he eaten?"

"Not since morning," Violetta said. "I thought… I thought your ladyship might want to take his meal to him."

Evelyn made herself continue moving, though her eyes narrowed. Was that an accusation? An invitation? A judgment or a show of deference? Did Violetta mean for Evelyn to drug the man again, or did she know Evelyn would and was expressing her disgust?

The answer was the same, either way. "No. Take care of it, I will finish up here and be in shortly."

"Yes, my lady." Violetta left her, footsteps soft against the paved pathway.

It was time she and the soldier had a talk, time she made sure he understood that his caretakers would know his secrets. Time for her to get a sense of why he'd come here. She reached for the sense of promise he'd given her that first night, but found it waning, guttering out in the winds of fear from *The Verity*.

Yes. It was time to speak to him, to stop avoiding, to go on the offensive. To control this one thing she still could.

She gave the soil one last press, forcing any last gasps of air from around the roots, and then stood, making her way back into the mansion proper.

She washed up and removed her overdress, then made her way through the sanctum to the sick room. Its door stood open, no doubt to lessen the stink that had built up inside. She watched as Violetta tipped the bowl of gruel to the soldier's lips, the man propped against the wall, breathing audible but even. His eyes were open, the pupils covered by a mother of pearl curve of scar tissue, blending into the striated grey of his irises. Even in the dim light of the sick room, when his pupils would be widest, she could see no trace of black around the edges of the scarring.

Good. His blindness was immutable.

Evelyn entered the room, and he pulled his head away from the bowl, tracking the sound of her skirts against the floorboard. He didn't find her entirely, but his face pointed towards her left shoulder. Alert, then, not just awake.

"And you must be my captor," he said, voice rough and quiet.

Violetta pulled the bowl away from him and glanced at Evelyn. Evelyn gestured with the fan that sat closed in her left hand, and Violetta sat the bowl on the small table beside the bed and left, pulling the door half-closed behind her. Evelyn waited, listening to the girl's footsteps. Violetta went first to Evelyn's chambers, no doubt to fetch the laundry. And then, down the hall again, until the door at the far end opened and closed, the lock turning.

They were alone.

"Your caretaker," Evelyn corrected, smoothly, opening her fan of black fabric. The air was close, and though the wave of her fan freshened the stink, the slight breeze was worth it.

"That's the other one," he said. "The one who just left."

Evelyn smiled, faintly, and found herself relieved when she realized he couldn't see the expression at all. "I make the medicines she gives you."

"You don't sound like a doctor. Or a witching woman. Who are you?"

"Your caretaker," Evelyn repeated, sitting back in her chair and looking him over. His color was better, but his forehead still shone with a faint layer of sweat. If she touched him, she would feel the heat. Perhaps a little shudder as the fever worked the bellows of his lungs.

"So it is to be a mystery."

"Your savior," she added. "You were lying half-dead on the road." *Up to my house*, she caught herself short of saying. If he didn't remember where he'd been headed to, she wouldn't remind him, not until she knew more of his intentions. "Would you have had me leave you there, to drown in the rains?"

"I do thank you for your roof," he said. "I prefer not to be wet."

He had a wicked tongue left to him. He sounded bitter. Almost angry. Not particularly afraid.

He didn't sound like a defector.

"As a thank you," Evelyn said, arching a brow, "I would prefer to know *your* name. And what an officer of the traitor government is doing in Delphinium."

He laughed and walked his scab-knuckled fingers along the edge of the mattress until he found the nightstand. But the strain of leaning was too much, and he fell to a coughing fit.

Evelyn rose and went to his side, easing him back against the wall again and taking up the position Violetta had occupied, tilting the bowl gently against his lips. "You are safe here," she said, trying to make her tone soft and welcoming. She didn't know how to do it. The words scraped against her throat.

"Am I?" he asked, after lifting up one hand to nudge the bowl away. She set it back down. "I find I'm blind."

"Injuries," she murmured. "Sustained from those thugs who left you in the gutter."

His jaw clenched. He didn't believe her. But he didn't accuse her, either, perhaps overwhelmed by the pain he was in. When he spoke again, it was to the wall across from him. "Will you be turning me in to your Judiciary, then, to stand trial?"

"If I had meant to turn you in, I would have done so already."

He groaned, trying to lower himself back to the mattress. She didn't reach out to help, instead standing, watching as he maneuvered awkwardly onto his spine. "You should have," he said. "Now when the servants begin talking, they will think you chose to hide me."

"The servants won't talk."

"It's a big house," he said. "Dry. Well-built. You have money."

"And yet I only have one person attending to you."

"I've heard other footsteps."

She let the wave of her fan be the only sound for a span of several heartbeats. "You're very perceptive," she said at last.

"I suspect I will never leave this room," he said, grimacing, one hand hovering above the fresh bandages Violetta had wrapped his abused side with. "But I also suspect that you are too soft-hearted to kill me. And where does that leave us? The Judiciary won't take kindly to you harboring a traitor."

"The world is not so bleak as that," she said. "In time, I hope you will come to trust me. To talk to me, before I release you. I have taken steps to ensure only my most trusted girl knows what you are. She won't talk. But the others will, if they never see the man who was carried into this house walk out."

"I could die in my recovery."

"You could. I don't intend to contribute." Her fan whispered through the close air. "When you are healed, I will send you on your way, clothed and presented as just a man. What you do from there is none of my business. I took on unnecessary risk by rescuing you."

"And what do you want of me, in return for this *kindness*? You could have immediately reported me."

"I want to know what you know," she said. "I am curious about the world outside Delphinium. I wonder what has become of it, and why a soldier would come here."

He turned his head in her direction. "I was sent," he said at last, "to find a woman. To give her a message."

Treason sang through her sinews, making her breath catch in her lungs. Sent to find a woman— and found unconscious on the road to her home. "And what woman was that? What message?"

"I can't tell you if you are not her. What is your name? I cannot see your face."

She hesitated, rolling the syllables around on her tongue. The temptation to know was strong, so strong. All she had to do was give her name, give up the safety she had bought herself with her brutality. It was simple. Easy.

Impossible. There was too much risk all around her to add more to the pile.

She retreated to the doorway. "No," she said. "I cannot trust you not to use that information against me. You're a clever man, you understand the position I am in. Your blindness is a blessing." He sucked in a sharp inhalation, as if she had stabbed him. "It's the only thing that will allow you to leave this house alive."

chapter nine

Two nights later, she scanned the many chairs and tables and reclining couches of Countess Urvenon's salon, looking for the black and gold flash of a Judiciary officer's dress uniform. Half a dozen men wore startling ascots of amber, but their otherwise unremarkable eveningwear took up all the air in the room, leaving no space for Pollard. One layer of tension unknotted in her belly, leaving only the roiling tangle of being in another's home, in public, under examination. Outside, her world threatened to go up in flames, but in here there was no Judiciary, no soldiers, no strange and staring girls by the side of the road.

"It is a surprisingly robust crowd," said Reginald Danforth from where he leaned against the arm of her chair. Evelyn spared him the barest of glances. He had attached himself to her like a limpet not fifteen minutes after she arrived.

That he was even here spoke to how the decay of the city suffused the air. Unlike her, all Danforth had was money. He had no title, and his estate was all new construction. Even two years ago, Countess Urvenon might have exchanged pleasant greetings with him on the street, but would never have allowed him to enter her home.

But rents were falling, and what was a nobility without its empire? The city alone was too small for all of them. They would begin feasting on one another soon, devouring dwindling pots of wealth. Danforth's presence hinted that it might have already begun. Those who formed alliances with and let themselves be ruled by the merchants would have their funds a little while longer, at least.

She'd expected Danforth to move off to one of the pretty young women who flitted about in his imported silks and lace, but he stayed by her side. Most meetings at the club, he was the best at forgetting she even existed. The change unnerved her.

"I heard," he said at last, "about the unfortunate happenings among *The Verity*'s crew. How many men have you lost now?"

Ah. He was here to press her position in private, where the other men couldn't see it play out. "Seven," she said.

"And is it true that the doctors are calling it a new plague?"

"Hardly," she said, refusing to look up at him, refusing to surrender any inch in uncertainty or weakness. "There have been no new cases since the night we put into dock." The girl had gone unconnected, and passed into nameless obscurity. "I have been assured that *The Verity* has been cleared to sail again as soon as her maintenance is complete."

"How very lucky," he said. "Is that the doing of our friend, Officer Pollard?"

He was needling, looking for a reaction. She would not give him one, not even stoic remove. She must be at ease. "In that he completed the paperwork, yes, but I have cooperated fully. It is a tragedy for my men, but not a concern."

"I hear he was invited to tonight's event," Danforth put in.

"He has better sense than to blow out his eyes with glitter," she said, shrugging. "He is an admirably self-possessed man. I am certain I have never heard his name spoken together with graft. It is reassuring, that we still have such men." A pointed threat—do not try to suborn him. It will not work.

Danforth shifted his weight, taking the message. "Still," he said, "what strange times we live in. I would think we would all feel much more at ease if the Judiciary were to do a thorough review of the matter, independent of the work Officer Pollard has already done. Just, you understand, to reassure everybody that we may continue visiting the same ports without fear of some… revolutionist plot."

"I should think," Evelyn responded, hands loosely clasped in her lap, "that the Judiciary, in such a case, should extend its review to *The Orrery* as well, as it came into port so close to *The Verity*, and had a much wider route. It is my understanding that the Judiciary is considering the possibility that this is not plague at all, but an imported vice new to the shores. My ships' manifests are well-kept; it won't take long for the Judiciary to compare them to what was unloaded. That should give them ample time to inspect *The Orrery*'s, as well."

It was the same maneuver she had almost made in front of Pollard, and from how Danforth's smile twisted briefly into a grimace, she suspected it would have been an effective one. Now, of course, he would have time to make sure to scrub his records.

But it at least set them onto neutral, level soil.

"Of course," he said, after his momentary faltering. "I will make my offices available." He pushed off of the chair and inclined his head to her. "I do hope your employees recover," he added. "The last thing we need these days is the loss of a good ship."

Because if her ship was burned for plague, it would be one less he could potentially acquire.

This was exhausting. She inclined her head to him in turn, and watched him leave, stiff-backed and annoyed. He'd be drinking heavily tonight, then, and she only hoped he would keep his mouth running strictly on the topics of imported wines and the turning of the season's storms.

Evelyn wanted to relax into her seat, but there would be no chance of that until after dinner, likely until after she had left entirely. Even with Danforth gone, there were eyes on her, so many eyes. It had been three months since she last appeared at one of these functions. She expected half a dozen practiced approaches from the fine women spangled about the room as stars upon the sky, their low-cut silks earning them hoards of admirers pacing out the boundaries of their skirts. The meetings would happen on the balcony, or in a hallway, or even here in the far corner of the room, opposite the musicians. And there would be two or three less-practiced attempts, young girls stumbling over requests for purging medicines, or creams for their faces.

She wasn't looking for new girls to help. Five years ago, before the coup, before the blockade, she would have supplied some of them. Most of them, perhaps, if they were deferential enough and seemed inclined to secrecy. But *secrecy* was a relative concept. That the younger faces at this party already knew to come to her spoke of the breakdown of *secrecy*.

Now she required greater circumspection. How many of these bright-plumaged birds would have already sung half a song to their closest confidantes about treason living in their spare rooms? No; new supplicants from this set would only lead to ruin.

She should never have begun this. It had started when she sixteen, freshly clad in black once more after her brothers' deaths, still believing she should play by the broader rules of the world. She'd been wandering the halls of a similar party, unchaperoned for the first time in her life, when she'd heard crying from one of the retiring rooms. She'd found a woman twice her age crumpled into a heap, sobbing for the bruises that blackened her throat.

Lady Amhurl had looked up at Evelyn's soft gasp, perhaps expecting to see her lady's maid ready with the powder to cover the marks her husband had left on her yet again. But it had been only Evelyn, who after a moment's uncertain regard fled. Fled, to her carriage, to her home, to her garden.

At the next party, she'd given Lady Amhurl a small glass vial of gelsemium tincture.

Lord Amhurl had been dead a fortnight later.

She's realized only afterwards what a risk it was, letting another know what she was capable of, but Lady Amhurl was practiced in discretion, and wouldn't dare incriminate herself. So, instead, when she spoke of Evelyn she spoke only of medicines, of fixes to unfixable problems. Nobody else in her circle suspected a woman of peddling bottled death; they made the easier interpretation. Contraceptives, cosmetics, cures.

Over the years, Evelyn's garden had grown. She hated the attention, hated the banality of the requests, but even as she began to live by her own rules, eschewing parties for the privacy of her home, she began to see the value in the power she held. On occasion, there were accidents. On occasion, Evelyn exercised her judgment. If a girl came to her seeking a potion to keep her husband's eyes from wandering, and ended up tending to a husband who could no longer rise from his bed at all, could Evelyn be blamed? Could such a girl seek justice without incriminating herself?

It reminded the tenuous web of women who looked to her for aid that to turn on her, to speak her name instead of whispering it, could not end well for anybody. It reminded them that in exchange for whatever cure she proferred, she controlled a new secret of theirs. It reminded them that she could not cure *all* ills, and that she was not a tool to be used. It kept them firmly at a distance, and Evelyn liked that.

The blockade had put an end to many requests, and she granted fewer and fewer. The remaining nobility, those who hadn't defected in the early days, as well as those who hadn't been at their country estates and were therefore now cut off from Delphinium, were a teetering skeleton crew. This whole party thrummed with an undercurrent of desperation. The smiles were painted on, the eyes hollow. The glittering crowd refused to acknowledge death lurking just out at sea, waiting for them, even as they all could feel the wrongness. They knew where to step around the rotting wreckage of what they had lost, how to keep their backs to it and plug their noses.

Violetta approached along the wall, drawing up just behind where Evelyn sat. "No sign of him, my lady," she said, confirming Evelyn's earlier search for Pollard.

Evelyn nodded, eyeing the glasses of wine being passed around by footmen. Her veil would make it too awkward to drink, or eat, and her throat itched with longing.

"Our houseguest," Violetta began.

Evelyn looked at her, brow arched in question. Now was not

the time or place.

But Violetta looked deeply concerned. Evelyn sighed and looked back out to the crowd, an invitation for Violetta to continue murmuring in her ear.

"What did you tell him, yesterday? He refused food this morning, and again before we left."

"You should have told me this before we left the house."

"His feeding is my responsibility. It isn't dire, yet."

"He is a clever man," Evelyn said. "He understands his predicament."

"Then he is angry?"

"I expect so. And afraid." Suspicious of the food, no doubt. "He is stronger than he was; bring him something more substantial than gruel. Perhaps ask what he wants to eat. He prefers you to me; he may engage."

"Yes, my lady." Violetta straightened up, looking out at the crowd.

Evelyn heard her soft, sharp intake of breath, and followed her gaze.

Countess Urvenon was crossing the floor to them, her motions graceful but unfamiliar as she stepped around everybody between her and Evelyn. She was smiling. Looking for Pollard? Her dress was a confection of silk and lace, her hair woven with gems, every ounce of her screaming that she was the Empress's favored niece. Two different times, guests tried to catch her attention, but her eyes were only on Evelyn.

Her bright, unblinking eyes.

Evelyn glanced up at Violetta, panicked. "Do you—"

"Her eyes," Violetta whispered.

That was enough. This wasn't her fleeting vision by the shops the other day. Evelyn rose to her feet, looking for the nearest exit. The door to the hallway, to the dining room.

But Countess Urvenon was upon them, and before Evelyn could slip into the nearest copse of conversing young men, her hand had settled on Evelyn's arm.

"We are glad that you came," Urvenon said, smile widening. "We had hoped that you would."

Evelyn swallowed past her rampaging heart. She wanted

nothing more than to break away, to run—but on every side, guests had turned to watch their polite dance. Evelyn had no choice but to play along. Panicked flight would only cause whispers of instability.

"Countess Urvenon," Evelyn said, as if she couldn't see the change in her eyes. "Your party is wonderful, as always."

Urvenon's grin widened into something horrible. "We are glad the body pushed her invitation. We were afraid she would let you go, on the street. But you came."

Her blood curdled in her veins. She began to tremble. She tried to lower her arm, remove it from the other woman's grip, but Urvenon clung to Evelyn. No, not Urvenon. *The body.* Whatever drug or horror had pinned Urvenon's eyelids open had divorced her from reason, from herself.

"Let go of me," Evelyn hissed.

"We do not wish to lose you again." Urvenon's grip, if anything, tightened. "It has taken us so long to find you."

Evelyn's expression rippled into a snarl before she could school it back to disdainful blankness. She leaned in, aware of being watched. "Urvenon, tell me what you've taken. You are not yourself."

"No, we are not her." The woman's expression shifted, grin changing to a distorted frown. "Don't you recognize us?"

"Your maid," Evelyn said. "Your maid, she took something, perhaps she gave it to you. What was it? A chew, a drink?"

"We've met you before, Evelyn Perdanu. Don't you remember us?"

It was a drug, only a drug; Evelyn clung desperately to that concept even as she hurtled towards the awful understanding that it was no drug at all, drowning in the riptide of the impossible. Her heart crashed against her ribs, as her lungs struggled against her corset to draw enough panting breaths to keep her upright. "Urvenon, you should lie down," she said, trying to pull her arm away, as if to lead her by it. But what would that accomplish in the face of this? Could she lie down and sleep off the effects? Rest, as if this were any normal intoxication? No.

Urvenon only stepped closer, far too close for propriety.

Evelyn couldn't hear the onlookers's reaction over the throbbing of her blood in her ears.

"We met you on the road. We apologize for distressing your horses."

Horror.

Evelyn wrenched herself away, and this time Urvenon—Urvenon's *body*—let go. The mockery of a frown turned to pain and grief, and as Evelyn ran for the door to the hallway, dodging around hemlines and couches, Urvenon let out an inhuman wail. Around her, the partygoers erupted in confusion, some running to Urvenon, some whispering frantically to their companions, some only watching Evelyn as she staggered out of the room.

Violetta was right beside her, taking her by the shoulders. Evelyn flinched.

"Get me home," Evelyn whispered. "Get me home."

She didn't dare ask if Violetta had seen what she'd seen, heard what she'd heard. The wail continued. If Violetta couldn't hear that, then—

"Come," Violetta said, slipping her delicate hand into Evelyn's.

Evelyn let herself be led away, but took one last glance into the ballroom. Urvenon had collapsed and had been moved to Evelyn's couch. Heads were bent together, maids thronging the room, Urvenon's closest companions trying to smile and settle the party.

And six heads were turned towards the door, gazes riveted on Evelyn.

Evelyn froze, staring back. All of them were faces she recognized, and yet all of them looked like strangers, bright-eyed and wrong.

One stood just a yard away, a young man whose wife had come to her seeking a tincture to make her conceive. He looked griefstricken. He reached out a hand. "We only wish to talk to you, Evelyn Perdanu," he said. "We can't bear to lose you."

Violetta tugged on her hand, and Evelyn stumbled after her, shaking, barely able to stay upright. The man didn't follow.

Other partygoers tried to block their exit, closing around them, asking Evelyn what had happened. She shook her head, hearing dimly Violetta making excuses for her. Urvenon had been talking strangely, had said something distressing to Evelyn, and Evelyn needed the peace and quiet of home. No, she didn't know what had happened. She wished Countess Urvenon all the best, and that the doctors could cure whatever fever had taken hold of her. She apologized for the hasty exit, but really, quiet was needed.

And then they were outside, the rain pouring, soaking them both to the bone as Violetta pulled Evelyn across the way to the rows of carriages, past identical cabs until she found the one that must have been theirs. She opened the door and tucked Evelyn inside, looking at her with normal, blinking, worried eyes as she lit the small oil lamp.

"Unnatural," Evelyn whispered.

Violetta nodded, wordlessly.

"This is not some drug," Evelyn continued. "This is something else. I can't—"

"I'll fetch the driver. Can you sit here alone?"

She wanted to cling to Violetta and beg her to remain, but she remembered herself. She touched the black gauze of her veil, smeared the beads of water trapped in its weft. She took a deep breath. "Yes. Come back, though, quickly. Let him fetch the horses on his own."

Violetta nodded, and was gone.

The box was close and warmly lit, and Evelyn shivered, hunkering down on the floor, wedged between the seats. Her gaze remained fixed on the window, half-expecting a staring face to appear inside its frame. She could still feel Urvenon's hand clasped around her arm, could still hear that wail.

What was happening?

"We can't bear to lose you," Evelyn repeated through numb lips. This unnatural thing, this spreading horror—it recognized her. It knew her. It *wanted* her. Before the first mate of *The Verity* had fallen into his stupor, had he begged to see her?

Had Captain Reynolds concealed it because it was so horribly wrong?

She was sobbing by the time Violetta returned, torn apart by the idea that somehow, she had done this. It wasn't just that her ship had brought something back, a drug, a sickness. It was nothing so passive.

Something had come back on her ship, looking for *her*.

And it was spreading.

chapter ten

"Close off the house."

They were the only words she could find on the long drive back up the hill, mumbled through her panic and her shivers. Violetta went into action the moment Evelyn was safe inside her sanctum, changed into dry clothing and bundled into bed. As Evelyn shivered and fretted, Violetta gathered the servants, sending some home and explaining to the others that nobody would enter or leave the house for the next several days. Evelyn expected there to be pushback, expected several of the servants to have been fired by morning, but she burrowed down beneath her blankets, clinging to the notion that Violetta would make her entire house a sanctuary.

It would not spread here. It could not spread here.

She slept fitfully, waking five times in the darkness afraid that she would find the bryony girl standing at the foot of her bed, watching and smiling. But there was only Violetta, dozing in the seat by the door. To protect her, or because she, too, was afraid?

It didn't matter. Her presence soothed Evelyn back to sleep.

In the morning, the rain didn't let up. Violetta dressed

Evelyn, then went to tend to the soldier. Evelyn paced the halls, forcing aside the memory of Urvenon every time it tried to surface from the mire of her thoughts.

She needed to pen a letter. She needed to alert Pollard.

Then again, he likely already knew. If Urvenon had dropped into catatonia the way the others had, then the news would be fire, spreading across Delphinium.

And what if Evelyn was blamed for it?

She stopped, staring at the door that led to the staircase down to the greenhouse. What *if* Evelyn was blamed for it? The fever had come over Urvenon when she had gone to Evelyn's side, and Evelyn had fled into the night. Too many people in that room had known of her green thumb, had reason to suspect its blacker side, and Pollard himself knew that she was connected to the first cases through *The Verity*. And that did not even consider what would happen if, still possessed, one of the other guests spoke to the Judiciary about *Evelyn Perdanu, we can't bear to lose her.*

Her wealth and the secrets of her supplicants had kept her safe so far, but Urvenon's stupor might be one misstep too many. The closing snare of the traitor government had everybody on edge, a pile of gunpowder ready to ignite, to burn, to explode. If Urvenon's collapse sparked that panic into full flame, if *she* were associated with it...

The Judiciary would come and break the defenses of her house far faster than any spreading horror. They would find the soldier. They would assume the worst.

She reached out a hand, steadying herself on the wall. She couldn't breathe. She couldn't *breathe*. She tore at her half-veil, scrubbing at her eyes, bending double to try to find usable air closer to the floor. None of it helped.

Evelyn staggered to her workroom.

She'd mixed the wrong balance the other night, and she couldn't afford to do that again, but she also couldn't afford to stop breathing from panic. The quickest answer was the poppy juice she'd had imported three years ago, but it had crusted to dust as she avoided it. She stared at the vial, trying to think. Something to calm her, to remove all thought, to stop the panic where it stood.

To stop it where it stood.

Evelyn stilled, hands braced on the workbench, breaths becoming fuller, deeper.

To stop it where it stood.

She could still fix this. She knew, now, that the catatonia was preceded by that wild fixation. What would happen if she cut the threads between obsessiveness and thought? What if she prepared a sedative that would free the mind from its fever, long enough for it to recover?

If she snuffed out the flame before it could rip through all the brush that fed it, perhaps it wouldn't recur.

That was it. That was how she would steady herself.

Evelyn went to work.

She had no poppy juice left, not in usable form, and there had been a prohibition on its import for the last fifteen years. But she still made note of the option on a scrap of paper. Past poppies, there was henbane. Chamomile and valerian, which she could add to every compound, to enhance relaxation and to take away the fire on the brain if the medicine didn't bring about full sleep.

And she could brew a tea of devil's trumpet as a last resort. It would distort reason, and might damage the senses for a time, but it would sedate without a doubt.

Beyond sedation, what other symptoms could she allay? Where else could she stop the fire where it stood? Something with cooling properties, distracting properties. Purgatives, on the distant chance that this madness was still triggered by ingesting some drug, on the hope that vomiting could shock the body back to its former state. Her mind raced over the options, and she pulled out baskets of dried leaves, took down withered roots from where they hung along the walls, crushed up seeds and ground them to powder.

She couldn't settle on one single preparation, but she worked through the morning and into the afternoon, setting down her notes and crafting as many options as she could imagine. She tried not to think of all the bright eyes that had been fixed on her in that salon, but she had to consider that the spread would accelerate. She had to arm the Judiciary as best she could. The doctors, no doubt, would happen upon a similar solution once they saw the disease in its non-catatonic form, but when would that be? How would they know to identify it, to connect it to the patients they already had?

When the smoke and fumes began to blur her thoughts, Evelyn went to the workroom door and propped it open. Violetta was nowhere to be seen, and so she let the air of the hallway mix freely into the room. She kept working, kept writing, sweat beading the top of her veil.

By the darkness of the hallway, it was near nightfall when at last she ceased her work, stomach empty and howling distantly for food. She packed her medicines into vials and waxed paper squares, organizing them with written instructions into a small wooden box. A calmness settled over her as she left her workroom and locked the door, walking past the sickroom and out into the main part of the house. Her offering would certainly bring suspicion down upon her household, letting the doctors and Judiciary know that she had a skilled hand at growing and processing herbal potents. Whatever rumors had gained strength after last night would be confirmed. She knew that some of the ingredients in her medicines would point to her less easily excused creations.

But she would bear it. She could bear it, if she were exposed in the service of stopping this poisonous, creeping spread. It would also provide a firebreak against the Judiciary's attentions, long enough for her to get the soldier back on his feet and out of her life. And Pollard…

She shuddered. He would attempt to shield her from this, too, she suspected.

Evelyn entered the sitting room, expecting to find Violetta on one of the couches mending popped beads from the gown she'd worn the night before. But Violetta was nowhere to be found, black fabric mounded haphazardly on the cushion. Frowning, Evelyn stepped back into the hall, casting about for any sign of life.

She heard no footsteps, no whispered speech, no doors moving.

Her calm evaporated. She clutched the box to her chest and hurried to the nearest bell pull, yanking on it and trying not to tremble.

One of Violetta's girls appeared in the doorway, dropping too deep a curtsy. She was nervous.

Evelyn's fingers tightened around the box a moment before she forced them to relax. The house was shut, and with the house shut, there was nothing that could reach her. Not yet.

"Where is Miss Fusain?" she asked. "I have need of her."

"In the parlor, my lady. With an officer of the Judiciary," the girl said.

Her heart stopped in her chest. Nothing could reach her, except that.

"An Officer Linden Pollard, my lady," the girl added. "The guardsmen—they didn't think it a wise choice to tell him the house was closed. They thought you should speak directly with him."

"Of course," Evelyn said, taking a deep breath. She held out the crate to the girl, who came forward to take it from her. "Take it to the kitchen," Evelyn said. "I'll be down to give instructions for it after I see to our guest."

"Yes, my lady," the girl said, and then hurried off for the nearby servant's stair.

Evelyn took the main staircase, self-conscious of the smoke and fumes that still clung to her skirts, along with the plainness of them. They were emphatically work clothing, and not the sort Pollard would expect from her. But what did it matter? It was all closing in, crashing down upon her. She hadn't moved fast enough, hadn't been good enough.

She reached the parlor door where it hung open into the hall. Beyond it, she heard Violetta and Pollard speaking in conversational, easy tones. With one last calming breath, she smoothed down the front of her dress, checked her veil, and stepped inside.

chapter eleven

Officer Pollard stood at the first brush of her heavy skirts against the rug. He was in full uniform, his hair combed back and pomaded. His expression was carefully schooled to a professional blankness that Evelyn could not read. Violetta rose from the couch opposite of where he had been sitting and retreated to one of the other doors, lingering until Evelyn gestured with a tilt of her chin that she should go.

"Lady Perdanu," Pollard said, bowing slightly. "I apologize for the lateness of my visit."

"I presume," she said, moving to the couch and settling down upon it, "that news of what happened at Countess Urvenon's has reached you."

"It has," he said. Instead of sitting, he came close to her, lips pursing. "I... I was concerned for your wellbeing."

"I am well, as you can see."

His gaze dropped to her lips, and she realized that he had never seen the lower part of her face unveiled before. "I heard that you left in quite a hurry. If you'll pardon my saying so, my lady, you aren't a woman easily scared."

She watched, impassive, as he settled on the couch beside her, almost too close to be proper. Even now, the impulses that led him to shield her had not been extinguished.

She must rely on that. She must nurture that. The thought was sour and heavy in her mind, but how hard would it be, to play the distraught maiden, overwhelmed by the impossible?

Not hard at all. She felt it in every inch of her, shameful and unshakeable.

"I could not handle hearing that wailing," Evelyn confessed.

"No, I imagine not," he said, then fell silent. It was not the silence of a man with nothing to say, however, and Evelyn watched him, dread growing in her chest. There was something else, something here that threatened his desperate trust. *That* was what had brought him to her door.

"Please," she said, and he looked up at her with a flash of pain. "You wish to say something. Say it."

Better to know the danger she was in upfront. Better to know if her fears had been correct.

He looked embarrassed as he dragged the words out of his own throat. "It... was suggested, by one of the witnesses, that at other times and at other parties, you have made deliveries of certain items to women of fortune." His eyes searched hers, as if he couldn't bring himself to believe it was true.

Evelyn hoped her own growing panic was invisible on her face. What she wouldn't have given for her full veil, to mask the tension growing around her mouth. "One of the witnesses, officer? But I can't imagine you were assigned to the investigation. Countess Urvenon's estate is nowhere near the docks."

"And yet you are the connection," he said, leaning forward. She nearly recoiled. "Countess Urvenon and several others of her guests are now in the same state as your employees, in the same hospital, with the same helpless prognosis. The doctors sent for me. And then I heard about that witness. My lady, you would not be the first in the empire to knowingly import new intoxicants onto our soil, or the first to profit from delighting the nobility with new and varied vices, but I find myself not wanting to believe it."

She closed her eyes. He thought only that she was a smuggler, not the apothecary herself. *Believe it*, she willed. *Believe it*, or else he would crack open another of her secrets here and now. She couldn't gauge how much the witness had said, or who the witness had even been. She couldn't know if she should lean in to this theory, or offer a smaller version of the truth. Medicines, she could say. Medicines only. After all, she had her box of cures at the ready.

But she faltered. She could only bring herself to bow her head and murmur, "Times have grown difficult."

Let him draw his own conclusions, and pray they were beneficial ones.

She heard his exhale and opened her eyes to see him looking down at his hands, frowning. No, that had been the wrong choice. She had to be brave. Had to crack herself open for him. She reached out one tentative, shaking hand and laid it over his.

His head jerked up. He looked up at her, beseeching. "My lady," he murmured.

"Times have grown difficult," she said again, "and so the women of the Empress's court occasionally come to me seeking cures for their anxieties. Medicines I make myself. No vices. No intoxicants."

His brow furrowed. "I don't understand."

Her fingers curled around his reflexively, as if he were a pillow she was grasping after a nightmare. "I learned after my mother," she said. "What to grow in a garden that could help ease the mind. Herbs, officer. Chamomile, valerian, sometimes a few things stronger. But nothing that would cause any of this. In fact," she said, catching his gaze and holding it, desperate. "In fact, I am compounding a variety of herbs that will, I hope, help Countess Urvenon and the others. I will send it in the morning to the doctors."

She held her breath, feeling stripped, flayed, the rest of her secrets perilously close to the surface.

His shoulders relaxed. His lips curled into the smallest of smiles, the kind that would have made some other woman swoon. She could almost sympathize, with the relief that flooded through her making her thoughts fuzzed and easy.

"Allow me to make a search of the house," Pollard said.

Her throat constricted again, and she ducked her head to hide the widening of her eyes. The soldier. If he searched the house, he would find the soldier, see the tattoos, be required by honor and country to report her. He wouldn't understand that. She couldn't explain that. "Officer Pollard, I don't think—"

"To set aside any fears that you are running an opium den out of your cellar," he said, and his tone eased as he smiled.

"Are you…joking?"

"Yes," he said, turning his hand over and lightly grasping hers, his fingers warm and lightly calloused. "And no. I do mean to believe the best of you. But I *am* worried about how this seems to dog you, wherever you go."

"Have there been more cases?" she asked, staring at their joined hands, unable to make sense of them.

"A few," he said. "But not many beyond the ones you saw yourself. And I cannot see how an illness *or* a drug could make the jump between your sailors and the nobility so swiftly and with nobody in the intervening space. It doesn't happen like that. I do want to believe the best of you, but your connection is the only theory I have. Prove me wrong, and I will be just as confused, but relieved to know it isn't you behind it."

The walls closed in around her. His fingers against her were still light, but they felt like a tightening vice. She could not prove him wrong. There was little opium in her home, but the rest… the soldier, the garden, her poisonous workroom? It would only bring on the noose.

"You look unwell," he said, and that pained sadness was back in his voice. She was losing him, she could feel it. She was not built for this game, could not use these tools to keep herself safe.

"I…" Her lungs seized. She drew her hand from his and pressed both her palms to her cheeks, forcing herself to breathe easily. He was watching her, taking in her weakness, taking her measure. She needed to appear strong, in control, the businesswoman he had known her to be.

Instead, she heard herself murmuring, "I am afraid."

Pollard's hand hovered by her shoulder, as if he was unsure whether to seize her or comfort her. Evelyn took the choice away from him, standing up and smoothing down the front of her dress again, pulling her shoulders back and setting her head high. "I apologize," she said, mastering herself. The noose, the noose; if she kept her mind's eye on the noose, she could prevent this. She had to fold her secrets back in, bind them tightly. "Last night was trying, and I find I am not much recovered yet. May I request that you return in the morning? I will assist you in making a full search then."

He rose to his feet as well, searching her face for... something. Guilt? Innocence? She watched him in return. Did he see her as the type of woman to be overwhelmed and need her rest, or did he see the calculating, shrewd creature of commerce who could, in a night, clear her house of suspicious plantings and prisoners?

She saw the moment he decided, perhaps before even he knew.

He bowed to her. "The morning," he said. "It was impolite of me to call so late. Please accept my apologies."

"They are accepted," she said. "After all, we usually meet in the dark."

"The harbor shift never sleeps," he agreed, offering her a small smile. "Please, promise me one thing."

"Yes, Officer Pollard?"

"Promise me that you will rest. You look unwell."

She touched her cheek, wondering if he could see the dread in her, or if it was only his concern at seeing her skin unobscured by black tulle for the first time. She *did* look unwell, and had for so many years. "Thank you for your concern, officer."

He inclined his head to her, cheeks coloring faintly. He was a handsome man, but not quite so good at his occupation as she had always thought him to be. But, she granted quietly to herself, he was used to dealing with sailors and tax agents and businessmen.

He was not used to dealing with unnatural creatures rippling through the fabric of the city like a sickness.

He was not, no matter what he might think, used to dealing with her.

He accompanied her to the door without issue and climbed up into his carriage. Once he had gone, she lingered in the doorway, waiting for her heart to calm itself and planning the way ahead. There was much to do: plantings to pull up and burn, or move into pots and place outside, for those that could stand the damp. And then there was the soldier. The soldier posed a problem, still too unwell to walk out under his own power or to leave to anywhere but a doctor's surgery, but now that he was conscious, there was a chance she could convince him to lie for her. If she bandaged him better and dressed him so that his tattoos were hidden, she could pass him off as Violetta's brother, here to be ministered to with her *medicines*. He didn't even need to be conscious, really—Violetta would vouch for him. Would protect her.

Evelyn almost laughed at the thought, hysteria rippling just below the surface of her thoughts. It was too much, but it could be done. And perhaps the doing of it would distract her, would erase the image of Urvenon's bright eyes, and—

Footsteps, running footsteps. Evelyn turned just in time to see Violetta burst into the hallway.

"My lady, come quick," she gasped out.

"What is it?"

"It has reached the house."

chapter twelve

The kitchen was filled with horse grooms, the cook, Violetta's girl that had fetched her to Pollard, and seemingly all the other household help she employed, save for the guardsmen who were posted about the grounds. They massed around something in the center of the room. A woman, bound to a chair with cutting lines of kitchen twine and broader swaths of fabric, worn shawls and the sleeves of dresses.

She was the other half of Violetta's hand-picked maids, a girl no more than fifteen. Her name was Iris Polemia, and her eyes were wide and unblinking, almost golden in their fervor, every detail matched to Evelyn's panicked nightmares. The moment Evelyn stepped into the room, the girl's head swung around, gaze fixing on her.

"We have made it this far," Iris said, and Evelyn fell back a step. "We are delighted to see you again so soon."

No. No, she could not do this, not now, not here. She wanted to scream, to rend her hair, to run screaming out into the night. Perhaps Pollard's carriage would stop, perhaps he would come back and see this madness for what it was, but no, no—

she couldn't risk it. And now this *thing*, in her house, and the Judiciary still to come at dawn—she could not bear it.

She must bear it.

Violetta looked up at Evelyn, fear shining in her eyes as well. "It came upon her half an hour ago, my lady." Violetta glanced nervously between Evelyn, Iris, and the gathered press of people. "While you were with Officer Pollard. She left the mansion yesterday evening, and came back just before we did last night. She seemed whole and healthy then. My lady—"

"All of them, out," Evelyn said.

Violetta fell silent, then took a deep breath and turned to their audience. "Leave us."

A few moved to go. The rest remained, staring at Iris, who looked as delighted as an infant, beaming at Evelyn, straining against her bonds.

"*Now*," Violetta added, an unfamiliar edge of fury in her voice.

They dispersed back into the bulk of the house.

Violetta subsided then, wringing her hands together. She shut the two doors that led into the kitchen, locking them before turning to Evelyn. "Are you whole?" she asked, softly. "You've been in your workroom all day. When Officer Pollard arrived, I—"

Evelyn flushed with anger and shame below her veil. "I am *whole*," she sneered, then regretted her tone as Violetta flinched. "And I have handled Officer Pollard, for the moment, though he will return by morning."

"*Morning!*"

"We don't have much time. If we are lucky, I have what might serve as a cure," she added. "I've been working all day."

"A cure." Violetta seemed to shrink in relief, placing her hands against her face. "A cure," she murmured through them. "Oh, thank you."

"We need no cure," Iris said, canting her head at them.

Evelyn shuddered, regarding the girl and the thing that rode in her body. The possession. It was in a girl who had access to her inner sanctum. How long had it been inside of her? It hadn't burned through her mind yet, but what did that mean? The sailors had been normal up until they disembarked from *The Verity*.

Evelyn went to the scarred wooden table where the other maid had deposited the box of potions, withdrawing one of the vials. The henbane tea blended with valerian. When Iris's eyes landed on it, her smile turned to a gasp and grin of ecstasy.

"That! That, which we desire most! Oh, but of course you have brought it to us, Evelyn Perdanu."

Her skin crawled, but she crossed to the chair without hesitation, taking the girl's chin in her fingers.

"Drink this," Evelyn said, and thumbed off the cork of the vial, pressing it to Iris's lips.

She drank it down eagerly, shuddering and sobbing with delight as the last bitter drops landed on her tongue. Her fingers spread wide where they were bound behind the chair, her feet stamping like a joyous child. "I taste it! I know it!"

Evelyn stepped back quickly, breathing hard. The effects would take time to overwhelm her, but the dose was strong.

And what if it didn't work? The creature in Iris's body licked her lips and seemed to almost glow from within. No creature would desire its own end, but if it truly recognized the taste of henbane, it would know what she intended.

"We slept for so long, above the great sea," the creature said with Iris's voice, taking a deep, satisfied breath. "When we first tasted it, we only stirred enough to follow. But when we landed on this shore, we could feel it, the roads and ways open to us. So much fertile ground to spread along. We knew we had to find this place that holds you like a mother holds her child."

"Silence," Violetta hissed, face ashen and eyes wide.

Evelyn slowly raised her hand. "No, let it speak," she said. "Why me?"

"You have what we need to grow stronger," the creature said, expression open and wanting. Iris's body strained against the twine cutting into her flesh, leaning towards Evelyn. "It's here, here in this place. We feel it. We know it."

"It's not working," Violetta said. "The cure, it's not doing anything. Give her more."

"What is it?" Evelyn demanded, even as she snatched up

another vial.

"If we tell you, will you give us more?" Iris's eyes sparkled, pupils constricting to bare pinpoints.

"Yes," Evelyn said.

Iris shifted forward, and Evelyn leaned in reflexively.

"The origin," Iris's voice whispered. "It is here. The start of ruin. We want to reach that beginning."

Evelyn scowled. "No riddles."

"We don't speak riddles, only truth. But perhaps you cannot understand yet. We hope you will, soon. But the medicine, the medicine! You promised us."

Evelyn hesitated, then uncorked the vial and held it to Iris's lips, watched her throat move as the creature sucked down more henbane.

The dose should have been much more than a healthy girl could handle, but still there seemed to be no effect at all from it. Evelyn gripped Iris's cheeks, tilting her face upwards and searching for the first signs. Nothing. Nothing. It was unnatural—

And then Iris's eyelids fluttered, the fervent light in her eyes beginning to dim. Evelyn watched the medicine work through her body, sedating and numbing. She watched as her breast rose and fell in slower and slower rhythms. She watched her eyes fall shut.

Evelyn stepped back, setting down the empty glass and keeping vigil.

"Will it be enough?" Violetta asked. "What is it? What will it do?"

"A sedative," Evelyn murmured, not daring to raise her voice above a whisper. "So that the fever might burn itself out without destroying her mind."

"Will it work?"

"I don't know," Evelyn said.

Violetta grimaced. "The things she said—"

Iris's breath rattled in her chest, wet and horrible. It pulled both of them to her, Violetta frantic but unsure, Evelyn reaching out to tilt up her chin. She set her finger gently against Iris's lips and nose, expecting to feel just slow, even breathing.

Instead, she felt almost nothing. Instead of her sedation following a gentle slope, it had careened over an embankment, plummeting faster and faster. Crashing. She was crashing. Evelyn swore.

"Untie her," Evelyn said. "Lay her down." She left the chair and went to the box, pushing bottle after bottle aside until she found the purgative mixtures she'd crafted. She plucked one out and returned to Violetta's side, uncapping the bottle and holding it to Iris's lips. The girl was insensate, unable to register the touch, let alone swallow. Heart pounding in her chest, Evelyn reached out and stroked the girl's throat — too lightly at first, then more firmly, until the muscles contracted. Not too late; she wasn't too late.

If she'd known to do this as a child, then maybe—

She pushed the thought aside. There was no time for pain, no time for her spiraling fear. "Part her lips," Evelyn ordered. Violetta reached between them and eased Iris's jaw open, watched with rapt horror as Evelyn dribbled another thin stream of caustic liquid onto Iris's unresponsive tongue. Evelyn stroked her throat again.

Iris swallowed.

Evelyn fed her more and more of the poison, until at last the girl's muscles spasmed further down her neck, into her chest, her stomach. "Roll her over!" Evelyn hissed, and Violetta tipped the girl onto her side just as she vomited, spilling bile across the floor and onto Evelyn's skirts. She remained unconscious as her body heaved, unable to clear her own airways, unable to recoil from the filth spreading around her.

But she breathed still.

Violetta looked up at Evelyn, eyes wide, brows drawn up in fear.

"It may not work," Evelyn confessed. "It may have already taken root too deeply."

"You've killed her," Violetta whispered.

Evelyn didn't flinch. She only rolled Iris onto her back once the vomiting had stopped, pulling the chair over with one hand and propping the girl's feet up onto it. Iris's face remained placid, empty. Before she'd lost consciousness, that light had not gone out of her eyes. There had been no sign of the girl beneath the madness.

Evelyn's cure did not work.

The walls were closing in. She couldn't breathe.

Think. Organize. One step, then another. First matters needed to come first, no matter her fear. Even if Violetta was wrong, even if Iris woke up, she might have the same staring blankness to her eyes. Death or the telltale signs of the infection— either one was unacceptable. Either one incriminated her.

"Pollard will be here in the morning," Evelyn said, not looking up. "I will need your help to find a way to hide the body—"

"Stop," Violetta hissed, breathing shallowly and covering her face with her shaking hands. "Please, stop."

Evelyn closed her eyes. She wanted to apologize, but what good would that do?

"We should have just sent for the doctors. I should never have trusted your—your—why did I trust you?"

"Because you wanted it to work," Evelyn offered, but the words felt hollow even to her. She stroked Iris's hair one last time, then rose to her feet. "She might still wake, if the poison didn't set too deeply before we purged it."

Violetta sucked in a shaking, uneven breath. Hopeful. Evelyn didn't want her to hope.

"She won't be the same, if she does," Evelyn murmured. Her eyes went to the closed door, picturing her waiting employees, huddled together, afraid against the dark. Their world had been invaded as surely as her home had. They would demand answers, before Pollard even arrived. What could she tell them? What could she do? If Iris died, then Violetta had seen her murder this girl, had seen her arrogance take a life that she might have saved. Evelyn could hear it in Violetta's voice already; she could not defend Evelyn for this, would not. Evelyn shivered, wrapping her arms around her waist, staring down at Iris. She'd been so *sure* about the cure—

Violetta interrupted the wild tilting of her thoughts. "If she dies, we say the fever killed her."

Evelyn looked up at her, staring, uncomprehending.

"That…that you couldn't save her," Violetta continued, voice quiet and gentle. "The truth, but one that doesn't make them doubt you."

Evelyn's breath hitched. "But you doubt me."

"I can be the only one." Violetta came to Iris's side, and took up the spot Evelyn had just occupied, touching the girl's hand. "The others don't know enough to keep trusting you, if they knew the truth."

Her heart spasmed. Violetta knew her well enough to still trust her? But what was there to know, that could prove her goodness?

There was no time to question it. She had to take hold of it and hang on.

"And what of Pollard?" she asked, once she had mastery of herself again. "He's coming here to search for evidence that *I* am to blame for all of this, and he will find a girl lying dead or as good as in my house. The soldier is bad enough, but the two together…" It was as if a horn blared in her ears, unceasing and unrelenting in its assault. She could hear her pulse rushing inside her skull, could see the Judiciary wagons outside her house, Pollard questioning her as to how this girl had died under her roof.

Violetta looked as if she might be ill. "I…I don't know, my lady," she confessed. Her eyes went back to Iris's body, the too-shallow rise and fall of her breast. "I don't know."

Evelyn could think of only one path forward. Her heart quailed. Her shoulders hunched in on themselves, battened down.

"We must tell him the truth," Evelyn said, bitterly. "That it has followed me to my home. That whatever this is, it's hunting me. It wants to be here. It will try to get in." She felt it circling, a hundred men with staring eyes, closing in upon the mansion. Suddenly, the threat of Pollard seemed so far away, so insignificant.

What was he, against a hundred staring men?

Violetta's footsteps broke through the pounding in her head. "No. We'll keep the household locked down," Violetta murmured, voice cracking, coming close enough to rest a hand on her shoulder. "And we'll have the driver take Iris to the doctors."

"They'll see the traces of my—" her voice faltered. "—medicine."

"Better that she die in their care and risk raising questions than for her to die under this roof and ensure Officer Pollard's attention."

Evelyn nodded, mechanically. "Of course. Yes, you're right. She needs to leave, we tell the staff that the fever outpaced our efforts and we are turning to the doctors, as we should."

"It can work." Violetta reached out to take her hand. Violetta's fingers trembled, cold to the touch, but her grip was sure. "What else do you need of me?"

Evelyn laced her fingers with Violetta's for just a moment. "Take the medicines back up to my rooms—we can't send them along with Iris, not without making the doctors more suspicious. And as for the soldier, when Pollard arrives, we must have his tattoos entirely covered. We will sedate him, and you must be prepared to vouch for him as your brother, taken ill and given over to my care."

"Of course."

"If your parents are interrogated, will they go along with it?"

"My parents escaped across the border last year." Violetta shrugged. "There won't be a problem."

Another deep pang in her chest, this time of guilt. *I would not abandon you.* It hadn't been an emotional boast—it had been a fact. Violetta had already chosen to throw her lot in with Evelyn, and Evelyn hadn't even noticed.

They would have time to discuss it on the other side of this, but only if they moved now.

"I need to strip out the more specialized plants, or else Pollard will have too many questions. And we must send the servants home."

It would be too hard to do what had to be done with others skulking nearby, others threatening to twist and turn with the spreading sickness. Evelyn shuddered at the thought, clawing her hands into her hair in a moment's fractured weakness. Then she forced them down.

"All of them?" Violetta asked.

"All save you. We will pay them, of course. But they—they must be gone."

"Won't Officer Pollard wonder—"

"Not if we tell him Iris fell ill." It was a feeble excuse; who else would send home their employees and divest themselves of fresh-cooked food and hot-drawn baths? But she was eccentric. She was terrified. He had seen it.

He would understand, if only she could think long enough, work fast enough, to craft the rest of the story.

They called for Violetta's other maid, who cried out and trembled at seeing Iris's body, limp and breathing shallowly. Violetta spoke to her in soft, gentle tones that Evelyn could not have managed, and the young woman nodded, going to fetch warm clothes to wrap the body in, and the driver to help bear her to the carriage. Evelyn watched everything, wraithlike and pale in the corner, mind racing. She followed, shoulders hard and tense, as Violetta led her out of the kitchen and to the main hall. She mounted the steps to the second floor, then turned and surveyed the ranks of servants arrayed below her, who looked at the pale-faced, lolling, white-wrapped bundle and whispered.

"All of you will leave this house tonight," Violetta announced.

The murmurs redoubled, then fell silent.

"Miss Polemia has fallen to plague. We will be sending her to the doctors, in hopes that they can save her, but it is not safe for you here. For your own sakes, please return to your homes. If you do not have a home you can return to outside of the manor, we will pay for your lodging. For all of you, we will have two weeks' pay in advance delivered tomorrow. Are there any questions?"

Some of the faces staring at her now looked relieved. Others, terrified. The rains were heavy outside, and leaving now would be to risk injury or worse. They might go to the Judiciary, let Pollard know to bring armed men with him when he arrived at dawn. It would have been safer, perhaps, to keep them all here, to lie and lie until she could lie no more.

But let the depths of the ocean rise up and seize her. She could not stay here, knowing she was surrounded by twenty other living, breathing creatures that could become hosts.

The only one left that she could trust was Violetta.

The murmuring began again, and finally, the cook stepped forward. Her worn face was creased with worry.

"My lady," she said, and she addressed Evelyn directly, daring to look up the steps into Evelyn's veiled eyes. "What afflicts Iris was no plague. I have seen plague before, in all its forms, and that—that—"

"Get out of this house," Evelyn said, voice cutting across the room. All fell silent. They were not used to her speaking to them directly, without Violetta acting as mouthpiece. But if they wanted to address her, then she would address them. "Out. Now. All of you."

"And what of you, my lady?" asked the cook. "What of Miss Fusain?"

"We will remain here," she said, "until no more trace of illness is in this house or this city."

Behind the cook, her staff exchanged nervous looks.

They thought she was mad.

They had always thought she was mad.

But they left her all the same.

It took long, aching minutes. Whispers filled the hall, and footsteps, and muffled sobs. Evelyn watched as the driver hoisted Iris gingerly in his arms, as much due to her terribly light weight as out of fear of sickness. She watched as the dying, catatonic girl was taken out to the carriage that waited beneath the portico, spared from the thundering rain but not from the noise. Outside, there was nothing but dark, wet shadows, swaying trees, the hissing of wind.

She thought she could see eyes looking back at her. She turned away, wrapping an arm around herself reflexively.

Soft footsteps beside her, different from the others. Violetta, come back to her side. Evelyn was afraid to look at her, to see if Violetta's trust had truly firmed, or if her mask was waiting to slip once they were alone together once more.

She was not expecting Violetta to murmur, just loud enough for her to hear, "What do you think she meant, 'start of ruin'?"

Evelyn shuddered, and took a step away. "I have no idea," she lied.

chapter thirteen

Evelyn thundered through the greenhouse, the towering windows that made up three of the four walls watching impassively. She tore up belladonna stalks and aconite blossoms, tossing them into piles destined for the hearth of her bedroom. Soil pushed up painfully beneath her fingernails as she worked, her secateurs clipping out stalks, her fists dragging out roots. There were easier, gentler ways, ways that could have perhaps preserved some of her vast stores, years in the tending, but she eschewed them all in her panic.

The start of ruin.

When Violetta had asked her what it meant, Evelyn had feigned confusion, but she knew. She knew, deep down where her heart struggled against the tight cage of her ribs. *The start of ruin* had apparently drawn this spreading horror here from the wilds of the sea, had called to the thing inside Urvenon, inside the bryony girl, had drawn Pollard's attention here with it all. The start of ruin lived in this house.

The start of ruin could only be *her*.

She had been just a girl when she'd started playing among

the plants, and she'd been just a girl when her mother had shown her how to pull the sweet nectar from the yellow blooms of honeysuckle growing in the carefully trained hedges in the classic, manicured gardens that had once surrounded Evelyn's great house. The wild growth beyond those gardens had been much less wild then, but just as unminded. She hadn't known not to pick the yellow blossoms that looked so similar to honeysuckle but grew upon curling vines, winding their way into the trees that her mother loved to sit beneath in the afternoons.

Evelyn had gathered a hundred flowers one afternoon, and, thinking only of sweetness, she had carefully filled the bottom of a teacup with the delicate sweet droplets of nectar inside each one. She fought every childish impulse to steal a taste, because her mother deserved all of it. She'd been sick for a spell, and was only just beginning to recover.

The nectar harvested, she'd had the cook make a pot of tea. She'd filled the cup with steaming water and taken it to her mother, who wasn't yet well enough to go outside, and instead sat in the parlor with her needlepoint.

Her mother had accepted the tea. Another day, she might have sipped lightly, only being polite. But that day, her throat had been dry and scratching still, and she had drained the cup.

Three hours later, she complained of fatigue and went to lie down.

By supper, she was dead.

And Evelyn had been there, her little fingers stained yellow, confused and terrified as the doctors crowded around the deathbed. The maids had pulled her away, but not before she heard them arguing in low tones about what could have caused the sudden death. It made no sense, they said. Had she eaten something? Drunk something?

And she had thought only of the teacup.

The maids sent her to bed, but Evelyn had lain awake, unable to sleep. It had been easy enough to slip out; the household had retreated to the kitchen to whisper over her mother's death, and they knew her to be obedient and forgettable. She ran out into the darkness, past the hedges, into the wilder woods. She went to the tree her mother loved to sit beneath, tears burning in her eyes, and she grabbed fistfuls of the yellow blossoms. But when she tasted one, there was no sweetness. Only a bitter wrongness that made Evelyn gag and spit.

And then she knew. It *had* been her cup, her childish impulse to delight her mother, that had killed her.

When her nursemaid realized at last that she was missing and came calling across the yard, she had hidden in a thick curtain of rose bushes. The thorns scarred her hands and limbs and cheeks in what felt like a necessary punishment. Evelyn had killed her mother, killed her with every painstaking drop of nectar added to the teacup.

They found her just past morning. They took her inside, bandaged her hands, and prepared her for her mother's funeral. A hundred times she thought to say something, to confess, but she would break down into tears with each attempt. Her father and brothers grew irritated with her histrionics, uncaring of her pain. And then her mother was interred, and she was alone, and that seemed like more of a punishment than anything else imaginable.

Now, with broken fury, she approached the draping gelsemium vines she had planted a year after she killed her father. It had been another punishment she had devised for herself, and nobody in the house had known how to read it. *The start of ruin.* What else could it be, but the shame that resided in this house, that had driven her onward to every other horrible act? It had been the excuse that had allowed every other transgression. How could a girl who had, at seven, spent a whole day lacing her mother's teacup with poison be anything but wicked? And why should she even try? It had been so easy to find herself capable of her first murders after that, so easy to excuse every drop of violence she'd distilled in her grasping quest for power.

She should have confessed. The rose bush had not been penance enough. Neither had the isolation. This, though...this was a true testament to her guilt. If this entity, this creeping horror from the sea, had felt in the woodwork of her ships and the tension of her sails the seed of blackness, the indelible mark upon her soul—how was she to argue with it?

Her own silence had been worst of all.

This unearthly horror, among every other person and plant and beast upon this world, had seen her for the wicked girl she had always been, and it had come to pull her house down around her. No matter how high she built her walls against the spread of it, it would find her. It would bring suspicion and fire to her doorway. If, somehow, she managed to hide this stain from Pollard, she would still have to deal with the whole of the city, with her competitors, with Danforth. Nothing would keep him from tearing her down, given the spreading rumors, the witness statements, the focus of the Judiciary upon her home. They would find her soldier, useless except to damn them all. She might fool Pollard, but she could not fool them all.

She seized at the vines, and tried to tear them down, but only succeeded in unbalancing herself. She fell to her knees beneath the arbor, tears burning in her eyes. Her fingers clawed into the soil and it crumbled under the pressure of her touch.

"Mother," she whispered, voice cracking. "Mother, I never meant to hurt you." She'd said it a thousand times before this moment, and a thousand times she'd had no answer, but maybe now. Maybe, with her house polluted by the unnatural, something would form a bridge between them.

Maybe she could speak apologies, and be heard. Maybe she could be forgiven, and this whole nightmare would finally, finally end.

She heard it distantly, as if from another room: the whisper of lace over fabric, the soft exhale of the young woman her mother had ceased to be. Her heart clenched, and she bowed forward, bringing her forehead to the soil. Its earthen perfume wrapped around her, fetid fertilizer shot through with fresh green and old roots. The smell tangled in her veil.

"How do I make this right? Tell me, how do I carve out the poison in me that calls out to this new infection? How do I make amends?"

She received no response to her plea. Above her pounding heart, Evelyn heard only the sheeting of rain against the glass.

Then footsteps. Footsteps, from just before her. Evelyn jerked her head up, looking for her mother's gentle, sad smile.

It was only Violetta, standing on the pathway that led out of the greenhouse. "The servants are all gone," she said. "And I think I know what that thing meant about the start of ruin.

"This all started the night we found the soldier."

chapter fourteen

"The soldier?"

Violetta reached out to help Evelyn up from the ground. "It cannot be a coincidence. By the time *The Verity* had docked and your men had fallen in to their stupor, he must have already been within the borders, perhaps even within the city. He has not told us how he came to be on our road in particular. Perhaps—perhaps this is the secret of his presence here. A plague-bearer, a carrier for that pestilence."

It made a certain kind of sense; more, truly, than drugs brought into the harbor or a punishment sent by the bleakness of the heavens to lay her low after so many years. And yet she could not believe it. It did not track, not entirely.

"Why, then," Evelyn said, "would it come for *me*, instead of anyone else?"

"It's seeking him out, like a dog to its master." Violetta was alight, frantic, hating. "Perhaps he was sent specifically to you, to take you down. You hold so much of what is left together. Without you, Delphinium will fall."

A flash of panic lanced through her. "A knife in the back

would have been more effective," Evelyn said. "It's impossible.
Violetta—"

"Perhaps it was insurance. He would come to your home,
ingratiate himself, and if he could not kill you straight because of
how you keep to yourself, then his infection would give chase."

"No." She shook her head. Violetta's logic made sense, but
then she thought of the soldier, thought of the promise still
carried in that head of his. If they could just get through this
night—if she could just put him to use—

But there was violence in Violetta's eyes, and a fierce triumph.
Her expression fixed Evelyn in place.

"And what would you have me do?" Evelyn asked at last,
voice softening.

"Kill him."

Kill him. Evelyn's own ambition and brutality echoed in those
words, but they were Violetta's entirely. The other night, in her
self-medicated destruction, lying in bed half-delirious beside
her companion, Evelyn had been so grateful that they could be
honest with one another. Now that honesty tasted sour in her
mouth. She did not want to know that Violetta was capable of
this.

Evelyn swallowed thickly. "And what would you have me do
with the body? We can't explain it away. If they find it, Pollard
will call for an inquiry, and they will go to investigate Iris at the
hospital and find the rope marks. They'll see the tattoos on the
soldier. We'll be ruined, Violetta. All of this will be taken from
us."

"We will burn the body, then. Eliminate all trace of him.
Pollard won't know to ask about him, and perhaps the doctors
will miss the rope marks, if they don't bruise badly. It will
be *better*. Easier, than if we let him live. There will be fewer
questions. My lady, you must do this. For yourself. For *us*. "

Evelyn could barely breathe. This was not the Violetta she
knew. This was not the Violetta she wanted.

"I will not. I cannot." He was so close; she could feel him,
see again his breathing pulsating in the walls. No, no, that was
her own weakness, which seemed now to bleed into everything
around her. Her weakness. Her ambition. Her desires. "He must

live."

"Why?" Violetta seized Evelyn's hands, and suddenly she was not terrifying but vulnerable, desperate for Evelyn's protection. "My lady, look at me, speak plainly to me. There is nobody else to hear us. To see what we do. He is dangerous and has harmed your house enough. You would have had your sailors killed. You let the girl die by the side of the road. Why is he different?"

"The sailors and the girl didn't have as much to offer," Evelyn offered, weakly.

"He has told us nothing. Less than nothing; he fears and hates you." She did not say *rightly so*, but Evelyn could see it in the firm set of her lips. "Tell me, what do you hope that he will give to you, that you would spare him?"

"I don't—I can't—"

The words would not come. Fear roiled in her gut. Violetta was right; the choice should be easy. She had made herself a hard woman. She had made herself a killer. What was one more body?

But it was not easy. That man, with his blackwork and his calm control, could not be her failure. As long as he lived, there was still a chance that she could crack him. Solve the mystery of why he had come to her, and armor herself with that secret.

It could not just be that he had come to destroy her.

Violetta squeezed Evelyn's hands, and whispered, "Why is he worth more to you than I?"

Evelyn made a desperate sound, a feeble protestation.

"If he remains, and I am right, what is to stop the sickness from taking me? From taking you?" Violetta's anger condensed to fear. To desperation. And then she let go of Evelyn and stepped back. Her chin lifted. "If you won't do what must be done, then I will do it for you."

Evelyn stared down at Violetta's hands, once calloused by physical labor but grown soft in Evelyn's service as she learned to work with her mind instead of her body. She'd always been the gentle one, had never asked Evelyn to give her a shred of her darkness. She had been kind when Evelyn could not be, filling in Evelyn's shortcomings that otherwise might have ruined them.

Violetta was not a murderer. She was not wicked.

But she had also aided Evelyn in ending the careers of lesser competitors, had she not? She'd been close at hand when Evelyn handed out small poisons to those who needed them. She knew that Evelyn could be cold and brutal. She had known that long before she watched the bryony girl die by the side of the road, before she heard Evelyn call for the murder of her three sailors.

Evelyn had needed Violetta's acceptance, and she'd given it willingly. And while Evelyn had foolishly believed she would remain good and kind, Violetta had also learned cruelty, growing up under Evelyn's ministrations just as the gelsemium vines above them.

She had to stay Violetta's hand. She should throw Violetta out of the house, for her own good, for the soldier's safety. But there was no way she could do that, or explain her reasoning, that would not also sunder Violetta from her.

"No," she said. "I will end this."

chapter fifteen

He was sleeping when she slipped inside his room and locked the door behind her. In her hand was a glass of brandy, warm, spiced with ginger and sickened with water hemlock.

Silence filled the close air of the room. She set the glass down by his bedside and took up her seat in the chair. It had been only three days since they'd last spoken, but the world had tilted far off its proper circuit in the intervening time. She searched his features, still marred by the remnants of bruises, still wholly normal.

Still full of potential.

But what if Violetta was right?

Every inch and speck of Delphinium had trended towards rot since the coup, a black working of the highest order. Had it been folly, to think it all caused by economics, instead of something much fouler?

Had it been folly to think she could still benefit?

He stirred.

Evelyn picked at the fine embroidery of her dress. She waited as his eyes pulsed beneath the lids, waited as the lids parted, as the eyes slid towards her unseeing.

"Who's there?" he asked.

"Your captor," she said.

He exhaled, slowly, and pointed his face once more towards the ceiling. "I see your self-delusion is over. Why have you come this time, instead of my caretaker?"

"I wanted to speak to you again. Do you remember how you came to be unconscious on the road?" Her voice emerged simple and calm, a firm mask over desperation. Before he died, before she killed him, she wanted answers.

She wanted to know what she was losing in exchange for safety.

"Some men punched me, several times."

"And had you been here for a long time, or not long at all? Were you in a tavern and they dragged you so far into the hills, or did some stranger accost you in your journey?"

He pursed his lips. Violetta had bathed him, but not gone so far as to shave the beard from his jaw. It was growing in thick and dark, making his lips stand out, a vibrant pink bloom. "It's muddled," he said, at last, easing himself up to sitting. "Though I doubt you'll believe that. I walked across the border; that much I know. And I know I hired a carriage in a small town a ways after that. You'll forgive me if I don't surrender the name."

"Of course."

"And from there, I came to Delphinium, and I remember stopping to have a drink, or perhaps several, with some sailors who had just returned from sea. They said they'd sailed upon *The Verity*. Great men, great drinkers." He shrugged, smiled ruefully. "I left with them, or perhaps with some other group. And from there…if I knew where we are, perhaps I could reconstruct it for you."

The Verity. The sailors had met him after disembarking. Her men, who had never seemed sickened on their long journey, who had changed so soon after arriving in that tavern where Reynolds had been. Her jaw tightened, the cords of her throat pressing against the high collar of her dress.

So simple. It was so simple, and not at all what she had thought.

He had spoken with her men, and her men had sickened. He had been about in town; perhaps he'd seen the bryony girl? And from there, how far could it have spread from him? That Violetta had not been caught in his web was pure luck, and Evelyn shuddered at the thought of her eyes, blank and staring.

"My lady?" he asked, and she realized he had still been talking.

"My mind wanders," she mumbled.

"Your interest wanes?"

"Hardly." She looked at him, and his tattoos, and the well-fed frame revealed beneath his subsiding bruises. He showed none of the rot of Delphinium in him. Life beyond the blockade was good, better than the slow decay left to her here.

Nobody would escape to a besieged city. He had never been a refugee. But she had known that, hadn't she? It was *she* who wanted to escape. This room, this house, this stalking death. She thought of the bryony girl, so desperate to get out of the city, and Violetta's parents, who had accomplished the impossible and left their daughter behind.

"Were you happy there?" she asked. "After the rebellion, were you pleased with your choice?"

"What choice?" he asked. His fingers splayed across his chest, across the stark tattoos. "Most of these are new. Five years ago, I was little better than a boy. And what choice did *you* have, really, in remaining here?"

Evelyn sat back in her seat, lacing her fingers together, her knuckles standing out stark and white against the sallow paleness of her skin. "Not as much of one as I thought at the time."

"Nobody much fled Delphinium or fled *to* Delphinium, and those of us in the ranks…we went where we were told. As it always is."

As it was now. Who had sent him? She could almost believe he was a pawn, perhaps even unknowing of what trailed after him.

He seemed so normal, sitting there, but such banality was a lie so bald that she could barely remain still. If he was afraid, blinded and captive in a foreign room, with an unknown captor and no true promises of safety, he gave no sign. He should have been frightened. He should have recoiled from her, or snarled at her, threatened or begged for his freedom.

Even stoic silence would have been less incriminating.

Slowly, Evelyn approached his bedside. "Your caretaker asked me to bring you a drink." He would trust a cup from Violetta's hand, distant though it was, more easily than one from her alone.

"A drink," he said. "And will you be drinking with me?"

"No," she said. "I'm not much inclined to it myself."

"A temperate woman?"

"A widow." Not the truth, but close enough. It was the old defense. He would write her abstention off to the vagaries of grief, along with the fresh brittleness in her voice that she could no longer conceal. They all did.

"You sound too young to be a widow."

"Fate is not moved by youth, in my experience."

"No," he agreed. "This drink. What is it?"

He was testing her. "Brandy. Spiced."

"I would think a woman with such a warm, dry house could afford the good stuff," he said, and heaved himself up from his pillows, swinging his legs over the side of the bed. She fought the reflexive urge to step back, to give him room. It wasn't just the way his muscles flexed in the lamplight. It was something else—confidence.

A confidence he shouldn't have had.

"Your blockade," she explained, trying to sound wry instead of nervous. "We've always imported the best brandies. Our soils here grow too wet for good grapes."

"You would know," he said. She stiffened, certain suddenly that her caution had been for nothing and he knew whose house he was in, until he added, "I can smell dirt and greenery on you. I smelled it the first time, too."

At that, she shivered.

He should not have been so perceptive, not so soon into his recovery. His mind was barely unfogged. But he could guess at her wealth, at her hobbies, based on the slightest details another man, even Pollard, might not notice at all.

"I've said something wrong," he murmured.

"No," she said, perhaps too quickly. She made herself take up the glass and sit beside him, too tense but readable, if she were lucky, as only shy. Reserved. "I just didn't think it was so noticeable."

"It's raining," he added, looking up towards the ceiling where Evelyn could hear the drumming that echoed through the house above them. "But you don't smell like water. Just dirt and green."

She didn't want to tell him she had a greenhouse. She didn't want to surrender anything, not even with his death so close at hand. So instead, she pressed the glass into his hands, guided it to his lips. "You're very perceptive," she said.

He didn't answer. At first, she expected him to push the glass away. Would he smell the hemlock? Heat threw scent more readily than cold; she should have cooled it.

And yet he drank.

His throat bobbed as he took a heavy swallow of brandy. No hesitation. If he suspected, he gave no sign of it. She pulled the glass from his lips, but his hand covered hers, guided it back. He drained the glass with a groan, then leaned back against the wall, closing his eyes.

He was still a soldier, enjoying a good drink after far too long.

"The house," he said, after a moment. "It sounded different today. Quieter. All the action far away, and the wrong kind. Different footsteps, too. Has something happened?"

Evelyn placed the glass aside and rose from the mattress, pacing between the bed and the door. How much to tell him? How much did he already know? His tone wasn't mocking, but she did not appreciate the idea of being made a fool of.

"Something bad," he said, frowning.

"I'm a very private woman," Evelyn said. "Perhaps I don't want you to know."

"Perhaps."

Silence stretched between them. Looking at him now, she felt something very close to pity. But she could see it, too, the blackness that was cultivated in his heart. He was more blameless than she but no less blighted.

And yet…and yet…

"I must know something from you. Plainly."

"Ask."

"You are not here by chance."

"That is no question. And am I not? You found me. You brought me here. I had no hand in it."

"Tell me," she said, heart pounding in her throat, "did you come here for me? Did you seek out my household? To destroy it?"

He was silent.

"You will not leave this house alive," Evelyn said, looking over her shoulder at him. "We shall have no more secrets between us. I am your captor and your executioner."

His jaw firmed, but he did not rage. He did not purple, or snarl, or even weep. He seemed resigned as he rubbed at his swollen, stubbled jaw.

Unnatural. Or simply good training.

"If you want an answer," he said, "you would have to tell me your name, my fine-bred murderer."

Evelyn hesitated, her hand for a moment on the doorknob. She could still flee. She could shut the door on this, eschew whatever secrets he still held, and pray that in the morning, her garden torn and burned, her guilt incinerated, she could start anew. She did not need to know this. She did not need to see her tragedy, her downfall or her squandered freedom.

She could remain a coward.

But she had not raised herself to be such. She came closer. Not close enough to touch, but close enough that he could hear her when she murmured, "Evelyn Perdanu."

For one heartbeat, the room was still. And then he began to laugh. He laughed quietly at first, raggedly, the sound creaking out of his brandy-warmed throat. But it grew louder, filling the room, and he fisted his fingers into the sheets, arching his back.

And then he stilled, and smiled, and said, "I would have been your way out."

chapter sixteen

She stumbled back into the hallway, but could not bring herself to close the door. Around her, thunder roared, rain pounded against the walls, and the soldier laughed so loudly she thought the walls would fall down upon them both. She was adrift in the maelstrom, its winds tugging at her body. She stared, fixated, at the soldier as he tried to rise from the bed. He coughed, laughter faltering. The hemlock stole over his muscles. He swayed, then dropped, limbs beginning to tremble.

The world became just a little quieter.

He'd be dead soon. He'd be dead, and Evelyn would be trapped. She had taken his secrets at last, and they had been exactly what she'd hoped for—but now it was too late. Too late by far.

She should have acted sooner. Laid herself bare, ready to destroy him if she'd been wrong. From the moment he'd arrived, she'd known, overwhelmingly, that he must have been sent for her, but what if she'd been wrong? He'd come too early. He'd come not under his own power, cast up helpless on the road. She'd been waiting for a man who would come and give her a message. She'd been waiting for a spy who would never give his secrets to somebody whose face he'd never seen. But she'd thought she could untangle who he was, prove that her hopes were right, find the truth by cunning, safeguard against every possible mistake and ensure that she won without having to offer trust first.

She'd been a fool.

An emetic. There was a chance, if she could make herself go to her workroom, that she could give him a strong enough purgative to save him. And then what? She had tried to kill him. She had blinded him. Why would he help her?

He would follow orders. And could he get her out swiftly enough, to save her from the spreading affliction?

And what of Violetta?

Violetta had known nothing of the deals, made at neutral ports, brought back in coded messages by her captains. Arrangements made, bribes paid. An invitation from the traitor government, a seduction, an offer—extended only to Evelyn, and no one else.

Help us strangle Delphinium, and when it is close enough to death, we will lift you out of it. They had asked for her knowledge, her capital, her ships and her relationships. And she had agreed.

She had agreed to keep herself safe.

And she never told a soul, not even Violetta. Violetta, who had been afraid at finding a soldier half-dead on the road, who had brimmed with suspicion but had trusted her judgment. Violetta, who had nursed that man day by day, and who had never known the right questions to ask.

Violetta, whose salvation had not been included in the bargain.

Evelyn did not move, fixed fast by her guilt, and soon the soldier lay dead on the floor. He looked no different than he had when he had been brought into her house, save for the stillness of his chest and the color of his bruises.

No sound came from the rest of the house. The drum of rain upon the roof softened, fading into the background once more. The soldier did not move. Violetta did not arrive to rid her of the body. Had she earned abandonment, too? Had her hesitation to trust in Violetta, born of her own desperate self-interest, finally turned her away?

No, Violetta would not do that to her. She would be hard at work in the garden, perhaps, or elsewhere in the house preparing for Pollard's arrival. Evelyn would go to her, and tell her it was done, and they would move forward.

She had to believe that Violetta had been right. That the timing of the soldier's arrival was still no coincidence. He had come the day *The Verity* had brought the first infected; surely that meant something, even if he had come at her invitation.

A punishment. She had already suspected as much, after all.

Gathering up her skirts, she forced herself away from the sickroom. She listened for any creak or footstep that might lead her to Violetta, but heard nothing. The garden was still and empty, as was the kitchen, the main hallway, the room she had met Pollard in. Frowning, Evelyn mounted the stairs, checking small side rooms, parlors that went unused.

Nothing.

Heart falling, throat closing, Evelyn came at last to her public study. She hesitated outside the doorway, afraid of what she wouldn't find.

She went inside.

And Violetta stood there, a vision in white. Evelyn nearly cried out with relief. But she was reading through pages Evelyn had left reviewed three days before. Evelyn frowned, going to her, footsteps softened by the plush rug beneath her feet. Violetta was not prone to nosiness. If she felt she needed to know something, she asked Evelyn to show her. She did not scavenge, she did not spy.

A spy. Her stomach twisted. She thought of the dead soldier, come to her deliberately, and she wondered—but only for a moment. If Violetta served some other power who had ordered the soldier dead, she would have done it before tonight. And Violetta was hers, hers entirely. She was the only good thing in Evelyn's life. Evelyn had betrayed her, but it could still be righted. This paranoia could only hurt them both. She needed to stop it where it stood.

Evelyn made herself breathe, her inhale sharp enough to be

audible.

Violetta turned to face her, eyes bright and wide and staring, lips curved into a small, delicate smile.

"Our lady," she murmured.

Blankness flooded her. She could only return that stare and fall back one step, two.

Not Violetta. Not her Violetta.

"I killed him," she whispered. "No, they can't have taken you."

"Him?" Violetta's face was manipulated into the semblance of thoughtfulness, followed shortly by surprise, then understanding. Sadness. "One of your patients! Here, in this house. Dead? We would have loved to meet him, first."

Evelyn could not take this. She could not bear it. She crossed the space between them and seized Violetta's narrow shoulders, snarling, "Get out of her! You are not welcome here."

"But you prepared the way."

"*Give her back to me.*" Her voice cracked. Her heart could not decide whether it wanted to pound or give up entirely. Evelyn saw the vacant eyes of the bryony girl, of the first mate of *The Verity*. She could not bear to lose Violetta that way, could not bear to see her stolen in an instant. She shrieked, shaking Violetta, hands clawing against her sleeves.

Violetta only reached up and touched her face, gently, fingers sliding up beneath her half veil. "We apologize," the thing inside her said. "We did not realize it would hurt you so much, to take this one."

The words cut through her, stilling her fury. She stared into Violetta's unblinking eyes, searching for any hint of her left inside. She found only the horror's unfocused delight.

"Liar," Evelyn whispered.

Violetta's thumb stroked across her cheekbone. "Your poison is in her veins, in her muscle and her bone. We thought you could not love her."

Evelyn pulled away, lurching for the desk. The creature watched, patient and unafraid, as Evelyn pulled open the drawer and groped for the letter opener. When she spun back to confront it, makeshift dagger clutched in her fist, Violetta's face looked only curious.

She should have been afraid. Just like the soldier, she should have been afraid.

The thought tore at her, but Evelyn made herself walk forward, feet digging into the rug. She could not let this *thing* take Violetta. She couldn't let it *keep* her. And she couldn't let it leave her unseeing, unfeeling, a barely alive husk.

But she quailed at the thought of what she had to do. The blade was awkward in her hand. Was it even sharp enough to end a life? It was not good enough to take Violetta, her closest companion, the closest she had come to a friend in all her lonely years. But Evelyn had failed her. She'd failed the only other person in this miserable world worth protecting.

This was the only option left.

"I'm sorry," Evelyn whispered, and lunged. Violetta's body didn't move, didn't recoil, and Evelyn crashed into her, bearing them both to the floor with a force that surprised her. But when she should have thrust the letter opener home, she faltered. The metal slid harmlessly against Violetta's ribs, slammed into the rug. Tears stung her eyes and blurred her vision, and she flinched as Violetta's hands wiped them away, sliding beneath the veil once more and then up, to the pins that held it fast. She keened, broken, as Violetta's fingers bared her face to the open air.

"Let us talk," Violetta breathed, and for a moment, it sounded like her. It sounded like only Violetta. But then she continued, "We have come all this way to speak with you. This form distresses you, but it need not. We understand now. We wear a face beloved by you; is that not the best outcome? We can sit, and talk, and we will be as she was to you."

Evelyn shook her head, pulling away. She fell back onto the carpet, dragging herself another few feet. Violetta watched her, unblinking, brows drawing together in confusion and hurt. And then she crawled across the rug to Evelyn's side, and gathered her, gently, into her arms.

"Please," the thing murmured with Violetta's mouth. "Please, allow us to stay. We will love you just as much as she did."

Evelyn stared in horror. Horror at the creature's desperation, horror at her own longing. Because, for just an instant, she wanted to say yes.

Instead she echoed, trembling, "Love. *Love.*"

"We know everything she once knew," the creature murmured. "She wanted power and strength, and she found the road to that in you. She first dreamed of being promoted to run the warehouses, work the numbers, but by the time you could see her worth, she was too much in love with you, and this house, and helping you influence the world. She began as a desperate girl, unsure of where or how to grow, and you became her trellis and her guiding sun."

Tears burned in Evelyn's eyes. She didn't want to know this, but she couldn't turn away. All those times when she had self-indulgently imagined Violetta's attachment to her as genuine, as true, as seeing through her veil and her lies—she'd been right. She'd been right, and oh, how sick she was inside.

If she'd been a better employer—a better woman—would Violetta still be lost to her now? Or would she be flourishing, living, a breathing redemption of all of Evelyn's faults?

"Tell me she hated me," Evelyn breathed. "Tell me it was not just love."

"She was afraid," the creature said. "Of you and for you. But she never hated you."

A sob shook her whole frame, and she curled up tightly in Violetta's arms, clutching the letter opener to her chest. She wanted this. She wanted to stay like this forever, to pretend that it was speaking the truth, and that they could play at Violetta continuing on.

But no. No, if Violetta had loved her so truly, Evelyn could not allow this to continue.

The thing made no attempt to take the letter opener from her, not even as Evelyn reached up and pressed its tip to the hollow of Violetta's throat. Her skin depressed at the light touch, but went no farther, and Evelyn wasn't sure whether it was the thing inside her skin protecting her, or Evelyn's own weakness.

They stayed like that for a moment that seemed to stretch towards eternity, and then she pushed with all her might, straight through Violetta's neck.

The creature jerked back in shock, or maybe only from the force of the blow, arms tightening once before loosening. Violetta dropped back onto the rug and scrabbled at her throat, fingers spidering over Evelyn's clenched fist. Evelyn pulled the metal free, and Violetta's back arched. Sound rasped from her before guttering out like a lamp, replaced with a rush of blood.

It burned across her skin, burned through the heavy layers of fabric covering her legs, and Evelyn couldn't move.

"It hurts," Violetta gasped, and Evelyn could no longer swear that it wasn't truly Violetta speaking those words instead of the creature inside of her. Evelyn sobbed and dropped the blade, pulling Violetta's body against hers, cradling it, pressing her cheek against her flaxen hair.

"I'm sorry," she whispered. "I'm sorry, I'm sorry."

Violetta's throat made a sucking, horrible sound.

Blood coated her hands, staining Violetta's pale dress, spreading out between them. Violetta's eyes lolled in her head. Evelyn needed to run, needed to be away from this place, but she couldn't abandon her. She rose to her feet, awkward and staggering, Violetta still clutched in her arms. She pulled the both of them down the hallway, remembering Violetta taking her to bed, remembering the walls pulsing with her breathing, her entire life unraveling around her. How she had been so close to losing hold of her life, and now here was Violetta, gone and dying, struggling to breathe.

She made it to her bedroom. Made it inside. Helped Violetta onto her bed, and bowed over her, crying.

Violetta whimpered in pain, breath bubbling. Her blood was a blazon across her chest. That, more than the coolness of a corpse or the frothed vomit of the dying, spoke of violence.

Violence. This was violence. It had always been violence, no matter how far removed the poison had made her, no matter how easy it was to deny the connection when blood hadn't been cooling on her hands. It had been death, wicked death, shameful death— but she had never named it violence, before.

The creature was silent beneath her as Evelyn counted out Violetta's dying heartbeats, as her pulse weakened, as her breathing slowed, then stopped. It was so easy to imagine that in those last minutes, it had been Violetta, returned to her.

She had to force the thought aside, or else she would break entirely.

Leaden-limbed, she washed her face and hands, struggled to shed her dress. Violetta's hands should have been there to work the tiny buttons, or Iris's, or her mother's, but it was only her hands going through wooden, rote motions: shed the dress, don another. Leave the bloody fabric on the bloody bed, and walk out of the room. Shut the door behind her.

And then the last of her composure shattered. She screamed and ran, senseless with anger and panic and grief, to her inner sanctum. She slammed the door shut and fumbled with her key, locking it tight, banging against the wood with her balled fists. She sank down to the floor, breast heaving, trying to master herself. But she became a wild creature of fear, even the close confines of her sanctum walls unable to comfort her.

She was alone.

chapter seventeen

The shelves and boxes of her workroom loomed over her as Evelyn cowered beneath the accumulated mass of her life's work. It had been in this room that she had crafted her poisons, and it was in this room that she had read and written her missives to the military government.

She stared at the sheath of papers on the upper shelf, carefully folded, locked away in the one room Violetta never entered. Letters and ciphers from the men who held the border, who controlled the blockade. Plots to take some of her ships, to let others pass, to create the illusion that she was just as beset as her competitors. She'd wanted that life beyond the border, strived for it, knowing all the while that she would need to leave her home to accomplish it. The harrowing of Delphinium would not be clean, and she could not be here for it.

And it was going to happen soon, if the dead soldier had come to take her away.

Her gaze dropped from the papers to the rows of poison. She saw the bryony, the cherry laurel, the aconite. The belladonna and the black hellebore she had used to blind the soldier.

She saw the old bottle of gelsemium, with its crusted neck, replenished year to year with each new harvest.

Had it come to this, at last, her path through life a loop, doomed to end as it had begun?

No; she was too much a coward to take that final step, had always been so, and even now, with her world in shambles around her, she could not bear to leave it behind.

But she was too much a coward to face the world unaltered.

Brandy and ginger and valerian. She mixed up the tincture with shaking hands that grew still at the familiar work, even as shame burned through her veins. She poured it out into a fine glass, imported from the other end of the Cenanthe empire, and she drank half of it with her eyes closed.

It was so similar to the poison she had fed to Iris. She set the glass down partially drained and wondered if it had been a gentle death as her lungs stilled, as her muscles went slack.

But this dose would only bring lassitude, a gentle distance. In the morning, she would rise again. She would find a way to rebuild, before the final fires came.

Evelyn laughed at the thought, sharp and vulgar, and let her head fall back against her workroom table. The small room was the only place where the walls came close enough together to make her feel halfway safe. Those same walls threw her laughter back at her: *Rebuild.*

The valerian fog closed around her, settling over her shoulders, running fingers through her hair. In the morning, she would make herself unlock the door, and she would walk the halls of her home until Pollard arrived. She would play the terrified maiden, home beset by plague, desperate to spare her employees but too frightened to leave herself. She would tell him Iris had taken ill and her medicine had not worked. She would claim Violetta had sickened, too—then run away, perhaps, to spare her. It would buy her time, just a little, but maybe enough to find another way out.

Except the rest had no explanation, and Pollard would never let her go when he found the bodies. She was running out of time. She would need to burn the soldier, burn Violetta, burn the bedding and the rug and her ruined clothing.

But bodies were not blankets and dresses; she could not reduce two corpses to ash in a kitchen hearth, in a single night. And she knew she could not bear to see Violetta or smell the reek of blood again.

Fresh tears tracked over her cheeks, sticky and noxious.

She could not bear this agony. It was the strongest, sharpest thing she'd felt in decades, and it pierced her straight through. She had thought she grieved her mother, but in the light of this fresh injury, that old ache was laughable. How could she have thought she still felt such pain for a woman so many years dead? Until Violetta, though, she had loved nobody half so much. She had never been at risk of feeling that pain again.

How could she hold herself upright alone? The creature in Violetta's skin had said she was the trellis upon which Violetta grew, but the reverse was just as true—so that now, when it was ripped away, she collapsed. She could recall a hundred moments, a hundred days, where Violetta had listened to her, had anticipated her needs, had *accepted* her without fear. Violetta had questioned her, but only to help her come to better conclusions. Violetta had nurtured her, perhaps not even knowing what she did.

She had loved Violetta. How could she not? Violetta had been clever and perceptive; attentive, supportive, never a threat. But somehow, Evelyn had never realized that her need for the girl was stronger than the pain and guilt she had born since childhood. That it could have been her salvation.

Instead, it was just another of her failures.

In that moment, she hated Violetta for being exactly what she had needed all these long years. She hated the creature for laying bare how they had grown up around one another, intertwined. And then it passed, and she was empty and bereft, cowering in her workroom like a frightened child once more.

She breathed in, a hundred distinct scents filling her lungs. The almond-like perfume of cherry laurel leaves, the pungent stench of baneberry, and all the rest, lessened by drying but not eliminated. They were as familiar to her as the reeking refuse of the docks, of the tar and sweat of her ships. They were more familiar to her than ladies' perfume, than the steam off a well-cooked meal.

Your poison is in her veins, in her muscle and her bone. Evelyn shuddered, eyes opening wide. She stared up at her workbench, at the bundles of roots and branches hanging from the ceiling.

Your poison.

The crew of *The Verity*, any of whom may have been given valerian tincture or compounded willowbark by the ship's doctor when they fell ill on their long journeys. Evelyn had made sure her ships were supplied with the best medicines she could afford, and some of her own making besides.

The girl she'd given the tincture of bryony to, to get her out of Delphinium and into the arms of a family that awaited her beyond the border.

Gentine Urvenon, who had come to Evelyn many times over the years, first to seek contraceptives, then to ask for more dramatic medicines.

Iris Polemia, who had taken ill with a boiling fever shortly after she'd come to Violetta begging for work. Evelyn had mixed her a tea of yarrow and feverfew, and the girl had recovered.

Violetta, who had taken no shortage of teas and compounds for her aches and fevers over the years. *Your poison is in her veins, in her muscle and her bone.*

The web spread out before her, blinding bright and undeniable. It wasn't just that the entity was closing in on her, that it was here to punish her; it was blazing through every body her garden had touched. Agitated, Evelyn clutched at the leg of her worktable and climbed hand over hand back to her feet. The garden. *The garden.*

The start of ruin. Something rotten in her garden.

With trembling hands, Evelyn fumbled with the key, pushing open the workroom door. The fog kept trying to pull her back down into oblivion, but she forced her way through it, staggering to the stairs that would take her to her greenhouse.

Beyond the glass, the storm pounded against the windows with renewed fury, wind howling down the chimneys, singing through the halls. She didn't pause to light the lanterns as she raced to the bower of gelsemium. She dropped to her knees beneath it, plunging her bare hands into the soil, and began to dig.

Foolish, foolish girl; when her father's body had been added to the family tomb, when her brothers had joined him, she had looked upon the stained, fat-slick remnants of her mother's earthly form. The bones were pushed aside to make way for those heavy, dead men, and she had longed to give her a better resting place. It had consumed her for months, until she'd hired builders to create this penned-in garden, her safe haven in the house that had been her father's.

The soft loam on top gave way to the harder, older dirt below, to the tangle of roots. Her breath burned in her lungs, but she couldn't slow, couldn't stop. Her fingers found nothing but soil, and so she moved to the right, trying to think, trying to remember.

Another spidering mass of roots, but these were longer, thinner. These were the gelsemium, the oldest rhizomes and runners. Her heartbeat quickened, until at last her fingers brushed the hard smoothness of bone.

Evelyn lifted her mother's skull from the earth.

She hunched forward, cradling the bone in her lap. In fifteen years, the gelsemium had broken apart much of what was left of her, but the skull was almost entirely intact. Evelyn traced the arch of her brow, pictured her blonde hair sprouting from her scalp just a few inches above. She shuddered, pressing the bone to her breast, trying to breathe around sudden tears.

She had buried her mother here, in this garden, where she had grown and harvested all her many medicines, all her many poisons. Evelyn's mother, innocent and dead by her hand, had polluted it all.

chapter eighteen

Her nails were torn and caked in soil by the time she was done tearing down all the evidence in her greenhouse, leaving the benign plants isolated and naked. Officer Pollard was a smart man. He would see the gaps, notice how the remaining trees and brush had grown in response to something no longer there, but she could not allow herself to fear. She was beyond fear, into the depths of horror and grief, and she thought she might stay there for a long, long time.

Her mother's skull sat at the base of a mound of uprooted gelsemium, staring at her from across the path. Evelyn couldn't look away from it. Was it enough for her to be removed from the ground? Would the madness end? Would at least one of the threats that bore down upon her evaporate into the ether? Alone, she had no way to check. She had to have faith.

Faith was so hard to reach.

Evelyn dragged herself to her feet and took up one of the baskets. She moved slowly, gathering up the stalks and blossoms, piling them all together. She'd thought to keep a few, but she had no time to transfer them outside, and no maid to help her bathe and change her sodden clothes afterward. She would have to burn them all.

The basket was almost full when she heard footsteps where they should have been none.

She stiffened, closing her eyes and trying to think of recipes and old shipping schedules, anything to will the sound away, and the panic that came alongside it. For a desperate moment, she hoped that they were Violetta's footsteps, that the whole of the night had been some fever dream. And then she hoped that they were Pollard's, come back because he had seen something that had made him understand why she was so afraid, come back to rescue her.

But when she turned around, it was the soldier standing in the doorway to the greenhouse, eyes still scarred but fixed, unerringly, on her.

"Our lady," he said. His lips were blue, spattered with dried froth. The lips of a dead man.

She should have locked the door.

She should have cut him to pieces and burned him to ash.

Instead, the soldier stood there, an impossibility, another problem, another disaster. Proof that it hadn't been enough to unearth her mother's skull. Evelyn sank to her knees.

"Why?" she asked. "*Why*? Why are you doing this?"

She eyed him, hating him, fearing him. She would have to subdue him. But how? Would the creature willingly drink poison again? Would it matter, if the body it inhabited was already dead?

And what of Violetta? She shuddered at the thought. Would she, too, rise again?

The soldier looked away from her, the first time one of the possessed had done so. He was staring past her, whatever was inside of him focusing on her garden. He surveyed the heaps of tangled roots, the pockmarked soil beyond. His gaze, such as it was, slipped right over the skull.

"We wanted to see this. To see you." He frowned. "But why are you destroying this garden?"

"There is a man," she said, slowly. "He will be here when the sun rises. He has seen how your path leads to me, and he means to find out *why*."

The soldier turned to her once more and smiled. "He sounds perceptive. We would like to meet him."

"He will have me hanged," she snarled. "He wouldn't do so, except for *you*. You have cut a swath across this city, leading straight here, and he will see this garden, see those tattoos on the body you've taken, and he will know what I am." She was on her feet again, fury burning through her, and she did not recoil as the soldier's body approached her.

The thing inside of him moved his brows and lips into an expression of confusion, of contrition. "You are the architect of our existence," he said, softly. "How can he hate you for that? How can he look on what you've grown, the web between people you have created, and see anything but beauty?"

"And what about the husks you've left in your wake?" she asked.

"A misunderstanding. We thought that they were prepared, that they were offered willingly. We sensed the bleakness, the pain, and thought we would remedy it for you." The soldier's frown intensified, and he settled one hand against her cheek.

He looked thoughtful.

"There aren't many left," he continued after a moment's silence. "We have burned through too many to reach you. But we can go forward in a new way. This man who will come in the morning—if you weave him into our lattice, we can take him. We can stop him for you."

All it would take would be to offer him tea or coffee when he arrived. Prepare it herself, work the slightest of herbs into it. Not enough for him to notice, but enough to lay the mark on him. The light in his eyes would be transfigured, and he would be gone, but she would be safe.

For a time.

But his men would see the difference. This creature riding in the soldier's body could not be mistaken for a man, let alone a specific man. She shook her head.

"He lose what makes him *him*," she said, backing away. The soldier let her. "The knowledge, the spark, the pain, the humanity. Everybody will be able to tell."

"We can do better. We can make ourselves like him."

"How?" she scoffed, biting back a hysterical laugh. "How could you?"

"We can see things, when we ride inside a body. We can become more convincing as we learn. Did you know how much your Violetta clung to you, how much you meant to her? Did you know how much she admired you? She never regretted her family leaving her behind, because you were her partner in all things that mattered."

Evelyn shuddered, shut her eyes. She couldn't bear to think of Violetta like that, couldn't cling to this sweet offering.

"We thought to stay inside of her," the soldier continued, softly. "Her affection for you comes closest to our own of all the forms we have moved inside of. We thought we could become like her, enough like her to ease your pain. We did not think you would hurt her."

"You had already killed her," Evelyn whispered.

"Killed? No."

"Replaced her."

"But in her, we could be her. She was not dead. She was transformed."

"You replaced her!"

"You plunged the blade into her throat." The soldier frowned. "You confuse us, but we will understand in time. We will make it up to you. Our lady, she was the closest to you—we had to take her. We would not have left her hollow, like the men aboard the ship. We only wanted to stay forever by your side. We didn't know that you could hurt her. Do you understand?"

Evelyn shook her head, violently, because she did.

If she hadn't killed Violetta, in time, would she have been almost herself again, an echo that was close enough? "Can you bring her back?" she heard herself ask. "Like this man. This soldier. Can you bring her back?"

"We cannot feel her. But bring her to us, and we will see. Bring her to us, and give her to your garden."

chapter nineteen

The world was quiet.

Her house stretched out around her, her sanctuary and her prison, and she could no longer hear the drum of rain upon the roof. The sickroom door stood open, and the signs of the soldier's death stank and stained the floor, but she passed them by without a second glance. She stopped only when she reached the door to her bedroom, and there she paused, trembling, hoping, trying to fight down the disgust inside of her.

Was this what she had come to? Bargaining with the unnatural to get a bare shadow of what she had once had? Just as she had never meant to kill her mother, she had not wanted to kill Violetta. A hundred others had been the fruit of intention, but not these. Not those.

She would do anything to undo those deaths.

The door opened easily at her touch, and she stepped inside, into the pall of copper stench. Violetta laid motionless in bed, the blood dried everywhere but the neckline of her gown, too heavily soaked there to turn to brittle crust. Her skin had gone pale and blue, and her hair lay in a tangled mat beneath her.

Her eyes were empty, inanimate, untouched by the perversion of the creature.

But where a gaping wound should have stood brilliant against her throat, flowering vines had knit the flesh together.

The vines bloomed in a riot of colors, small-petaled blossoms with long stamens, casting a fine dusting of pollen across the bed. Evelyn approached, heart in her throat. She knelt beside the bed and reached out with her practiced fingers, stroking the petals, inspecting the leaves. The features belonged to no plant she knew, and they seemed to possess a hundred conflicting traits. Some stems were knobbed, some smooth, some dense like fungus. The flowers, too, differed in tiny ways, and she saw in each echoes of plants she had fed Violetta, had fed herself, had fed Delphinium.

A hundred thousand traces of her, fingerprinted on Violetta's flesh.

She tried to disentangle the stems and roots from Violetta, but they refused to give. The plants shivered at her touch and released a heady, melancholy perfume. Unnatural; this was unnatural, too. But it had to mean something, something about the garden, the start of ruin.

This wasn't just violence. It was something else. Something new. Something she couldn't understand.

"I am sorry," Evelyn said, lifting her hand to cup Violetta's face. "I am so sorry."

Violetta did not respond.

She waited for a flare of gold to steal over her eyes, or even that familiar emptiness, but there was only the blankness of death.

Biting down a sob, Evelyn lifted Violetta into her arms. Violetta was a small woman, but Evelyn was exhausted, and she struggled to bear Violetta's weight out into the hall. Her every step was an insult, unsteady and unworthy. But she made it back down to the garden despite the weakness of her muscles. She reached where she had placed her mother's skull, and where the soldier still stood, and she laid Violetta down between them.

The moon broke from behind the clouds. Silver light slid into the dark places of the greenhouse. And where there should have been gaps, she saw leaves, stems, blossoms. Beneath her feet, all around her, the soil in the beds shifted. In the gaps left bare by her destruction, new growth shot up. It came from shreds of root left behind, fragments of leaf she had not yet turned into the soil. Her hellebore strained up from the ground, pointed leaves growing lush and sheltering over fresh blossoms. Foxglove spiraled upwards, sprouting a hundred new screaming flowers, and behind them spread gelsemium vines, spidering out across the greenhouse to throw out saplings, climb walls, scale doorways.

The plants were so close to the ones she had known, that had comforted her all her life, but she knew them too well to think them strong and healthy. Some were sickly pale; others sparsely grown, erupting too fast to remain alive for long. Sap oozed from stems that splintered under their own weight. Roots pushed up from the soil like bulbous maggots, the ground unable to contain them. The gelsemium multiplied past all reason, siphoning vitality from everything it touched, its myriad hosts becoming drawn and limp before her eyes.

"What are you doing?" she asked.

The soldier smiled. "Spreading. Spreading, in a new way."

She looked down at Violetta, then, crouching beside her, touched the blossoms. Each flower differed, but the petals were evenly formed, the stems strong, the leaves gleaming in the low light. "Are these yours, too?"

The soldier's smile twisted into something else, something wrong. "Only weeds," the soldier said. "Give her to the garden." Something in its tone had shifted.

"Will it bring her back?"

The soldier did not speak.

"These flowers," she said. "These flowers, what are they?"

"Poison," the soldier said, and there was no delight in the word. No wonder. No hunger. "She is gone. She is gone, our lady."

"No," she said, scowling. "No, that was not the bargain. I have brought her to you. I have never offered you anybody with full knowledge until *her*, and you say she is gone? *No.* Take her. Now. Bring her back to me."

"We cannot feel her," the creature said. The soldier bared his teeth, for only a moment, as if angry.

She had never seen it angry before. And her anger matched the creature's, swirling inside her heart, hot and inflamed. But she would not beg, and she could see no other way to force the thing.

And what did it mean, that Violetta had sprouted after death, while the soldier stood before her now?

It meant that there was no way to make amends. There was no way to playact, to pretend Violetta was back and that Evelyn had not betrayed her. It meant that there was nothing left for her here except the gallows.

The fight inside of her died back. Her heart broke. Relief crept forward, too; could she have truly born seeing that golden light in Violetta's gaze once more?

"Take me out of the city," she whispered, subsiding.

"Our lady?"

She looked at the soldier's body, at his tattoos. "You say you can play a role? If you cannot play Violetta's, then play this man's. Take me away, somewhere safe." Because the only alternative was death, and she knew she was too cowardly to take that option. She always had been. But she could not remain here, her handiwork arrayed around her, her night's labors undone in an instant.

"We could do this for you," the soldier said, and she could have screamed from the surge of guilt and relief that flooded her, working into the tiniest crevices of her skull. She did not want to leave this house, but her safety was gone. Gone, forever. This house was no longer the fortress she had built.

"But there is no need, our lady."

Evelyn stilled. "There is every need."

"We feel your hand on this city, on the wind, in the soil. You have touched so many; we have found them. But there are others, too. Others, poisoned by your influence. We feel it, the spread of rot. We can use it. We will change them, as we are changing this garden now."

She could see behind the soldier the lights of the city below, and they looked like eyes, winking, watching, golden and staring.

A hundred eyes, a thousand. All of Delphinium, bewitched.

Blood drained from her face. "No. No, that is—no, the Empress is foolish, and this city is dying, but I—I—"

I am responsible.

"Your rescuers would have caged you, made you reliant on them for every scrap," the soldier continued, and he went down onto his knees before her, the supplicant. "You have killed for less. You grow your freedom. You do not need to rely on us; we will rely on you."

Outside, the ground appeared to tremble. She could have sworn she heard the sound of green things growing, of soil shifting, of the swell of ripe fruit.

"We will make for you a home. A home which loves you, accepts you, sees all of you and will never seek to punish you for it. It is the least we can do for you, our lady. We have lived so long adrift, without a medium in which to take root and spread, but you have provided it for us. A whole city, a whole, closed world, that will serve you. A better world."

A whole world that will love you. It was tempting, just as Violetta resurrected to a half life had been tempting. A world where she no longer had to guard herself, a world where she could unspool the tangled knot that was her beating heart. A whole world like that night when Violetta had found her, addled and mad, and had stayed by her side. A world where she could act not out of fear, but out of want. Desire.

But the temptation faded as quickly as it had bloomed, strangled by the memory of Violetta's blood pooling in her mouth, drowning her. The very temptation proved Evelyn didn't deserve that world. She'd barely deserved to exist within these walls that she'd built to protect herself, and now she had destroyed it all, killed again the one person who made her feel as if she could be forgiven.

"We can give you your dreams," the soldier said. "We cannot bring *her* back, and for that we are sorry. But we can do so much more. We are doing so much more."

Evelyn laughed, weakly. "I don't want this," she said. "I don't want any of this."

"You have created the world in which you live, but it is

imperfect. Let us help you."

"No," she whispered.

"You would have let them all die anyway, once you left them behind for the border crossing," the soldier said, driving a burning stake through Evelyn's chest. "We do not see the difference."

"What are you?" she asked.

Silence.

Then the soldier reached out and took both of Evelyn's hands in his. His thumbs stroked the pinprick scars that traced over her knuckles. "We are an old thing, and a new thing," the creature said. "We... are not sure what we are. But we saw the first of your poisoned men, and we knew that to fill him would be to let ourselves out of the darkness. We are a child, our lady. Would you end us before we can begin?"

"You are a pestilence," Evelyn said. "You are... you are like me. You take and take, because you fear if you cease to take, you will lose all that you are. You can't exist without the greater world. I grew off their excesses, their weaknesses, their structures and needs and movements." All true. All hated facts, all undeniable. Her throat was dry and tight. "Without them, I will be nothing."

"Please believe us," the creature murmured. "With *us*, you are everything."

Evelyn looked away, back to Violetta, back to her mother's skull beside her. From the fine cracks in the bone, new growth sprouted, each stem supple, each sinuous root careful to settle where it might be sustained. Small tendrils curled into Evelyn's skirts, brushed against her wrists. This new verdance did not erupt and struggle and seize, like the strange sprawl of the garden, but beckoned instead. As if it were offering to pull the weight of her shame back into the soil. Away from the cruel future before her.

Beneath her, the city writhed. By morning, would there even be a Judiciary? Would there be any threat left at all? Or would the whole of Delphinium be made a great garden, with nobody left to threaten her?

But without Violetta there to remind her she was human, she

wanted none of it.

From her mother's skull bloomed new flowers, the same strange array as sprawled from Violetta's throat, the same myriad of influences. *Poison*, the creature had called it. *Weeds.* They beckoned.

Trembling, Evelyn reached out and plucked one.

Cupped in her palm, its color brightened, almost pulsing. It frightened her, made her think of staring eyes and deep obsession, but the soldier moved, as if to stop her, and that was enough. She pulled its stamen out, revealing a bead of shimmering nectar. Before she could think twice, she touched it to her tongue.

The world exploded.

It happened in a wave, a flash, an eternity. Evelyn's mind quickened, spread, and she could see everything around her, she could see the whole of the city and the smallness of the tiniest seed at once. A thousand glowing threads, each singing to each other and to her, straining to reach her, straining to conquer the world. Iris was in there, desperate for a home, learning to please. Urvenon, in her gowns, and her sailors on the rocking seas. The city, rotting, dying, deliquescing, giving over to the fungal spiderings of the creature.

The city, waking up. Shifting. Transforming.

And then it all compressed, roaring into her body, the frailty of her limbs and the exhaustion of her organs. Her stomach roiled. Her hands trembled. She pitched forward onto the cold softness of Violetta, the dampness of the soil. Vines twined around her, and she cried out, unseeing, seeing all. Above her, she heard the soldier moving, wailing. What was happening? What was becoming?

A thousand voices chorused in her head, and she wept. She trembled and spasmed, and wondered what would happen next, if she would lose all thought, or see herself rise on puppet strings.

But neither happened. Instead, she felt a keening that was not her own. Words, tumbling words. *Why? How could you? We loved you. We loved you first.*

No; no, the woman whose bones she cradled in desperate hands had loved her first. The woman whose corpse now pillowed Evelyn's thrashing body had loved her last. This thing—this thing had not known her, had seen only the fragments of herself that Evelyn hated most.

Evelyn's limbs grew leaden, and though they ceased their spasms, it was all she could do to push herself up on her arms, to stop crushing Violetta. She trembled, her gaze blurring and focusing too fast to think. She lifted one hand to brush over the blossoms at Violetta's throat, and their heady smell filled the air.

The soldier had not grown these. Iris had not grown there. It was Violetta, and her mother, and they were different, somehow. They were different.

She had made them different, made them *more*, and though she did not deserve their love, they had provided her absolution.

Her heart raced in an uneven rhythm, and Evelyn had toed the paths of death often enough to know that the nectar had been poison. It was not just the strange surging of awareness within her, but the hitching of her breath, the tightening of her muscles. But if it was going to be over, then it was over not out of cowardice, but out of bravery. Bravery, to reject temptation, to reject another escape. She felt inside of her the combined whole of the network of suffering and obsession she had given life to, and though it struggled, it had no path left to it. Whatever had grown from Violetta and her mother, it was as much an antidote as a poison.

She did not close her eyes as she brought her lips to Violetta's, a final goodbye.

And then, between her, something new. The flowers in Violetta's throat responded to the poison on her lips. Beneath her, the body stirred. Familiar hands reached up to hold her, to ease her over onto her side. She gasped for breath as Violetta peered at her, frowning, then touched the blossoms at her throat in confusion.

Violetta. *Alive.*

Evelyn had stumbled into salvation, of a kind. As if from far away, she heard her mother's voice, whispering: *Why did you ever blame yourself?*

"Evelyn," Violetta said, bending close. "My lady, Evelyn. What has happened?"

Did she still have words, or a voice to speak them with? She wasn't sure. She was so heavy, so full of impossibilities, and she wept.

The soldier's body lay still beside them. If Evelyn concentrated, she could hear his voice, see the face of his commanders. So much knowledge, so much hope, and fear, and hatred of her, and bleak amusement at how fate had crossed him. But he, too, was free now. And beyond him, the city had ceased its roiling. The horrors were over, contained in her soul.

"I have ended it," she whispered.

The garden stirred around her, one last time, and Violetta stumbled back, pulling herself from the earth. Evelyn did not fight; she felt roots twine around her arms, in between her fingers as she curled against the cool, damp soil, pulling the fragments of her mother's skull against her chest. It eased something inside of her, something old and vicious, and she felt herself smiling. She was glad the end had come this way. She was glad to be in her garden.

She was glad to no longer be afraid.

In the chambers of her heart, she felt something split open and begin to grow, and she gave herself over to it.

epilogue

Violetta Fusain sat vigil in the garden until dawn. She watched as roots drew the soldier's body down beside Lady Perdanu's, and as life erupted from her employer, bright green life, a tree growing so fast from her heart that Violetta could hear a great noise coming from it. She watched its boughs spread over the garden, and she watched its roots bury the evidence of what had happened.

When the garden was once again still and the house was empty, and she could still breathe despite the distant memory of metal piercing her throat, she rose from the graveside and went back into the house.

She found the door to Evelyn's workroom, and after a moment's guilt, she stepped inside. She examined the medicines and poisons, scrawled notes and recipes, and the sheaf of paper detailing treason. Her heart gave an unwelcome pang as she burned every page, turning the evidence to ash. The only page she spared was on heavy stock and notarized three times.

It was a will, leaving Perdanu shipping to Violetta Fusain, dated nearly a year ago.

In Evelyn's room, Violetta stripped the blood-soaked bed and hid the linens. She had no time to burn so much material, not with Pollard due to arrive at any moment. Instead, she changed into one of Evelyn's high-collared dresses. Her mourning black now felt more appropriate than Violetta's own delicate white, and the cut of the dress smothered the flowers at her throat, multi-hued blossoms that hurt like her own flesh when she tried to pluck them out.

Later. Later, she would learn what had been made of her.

She busied herself in the sickroom, next, removing every trace of the soldier, and then the kitchen. There was so much to be done, and there should have been no time at all to do it.

And yet the day moved on.

When Officer Pollard arrived at last, the sun was beginning to set, and he was alone. He came with no soldiers, no Judiciary men, not even a driver, and he sagged heavily on the front steps even as she opened the door to him. They stared at each other for a long time, and then, at last, Violetta looked beyond the house, to the city below.

Smoke blanketed the valley, and the harbor was full of liveried ships, their scarlet sails undeniable even at a distance.

The rebel navy had arrived. And they had won, in under a day.

"How?" she asked, softly.

"Black magic," Pollard replied. "A living nightmare. The city overrun by the afflicted, and a forest growing up in city streets. I am so relieved to find you spared."

Violetta said nothing, and at last Pollard noticed the inky darkness of her gown.

He squeezed shut his eyes and bowed his head.

"The Empress has surrendered," he said, after silence had stretched long enough between them that it gained a physical presence. "They are saying we are lucky. That the government may be fallen, that the wealthy may have all gone mad or catatonic, but at least the rest of us remain. There was no need to lay siege, to starve us out, to burn the city down. So we are lucky."

"Strange," Violetta said. "I do not feel lucky."

But even as she said it, she knew that was not true. Escape was no longer necessary. And with Evelyn's will, if it was respected, she could build anew. Delphinium had survived, changed hands to a less covetous, more reasonable government. What did it matter to her, if the Empress still ruled the city, as long as she had bread? As long as she had her ships, and this house? Her new masters had wanted to make use of Evelyn Perdanu; they could make use of her just as well.

"Where is your lady?" Pollard asked at last.

"In the garden," Violetta said, without thinking. She hesitated only a moment, then stepped back to let him in. She had cleansed the house. There was little left to fear, except for that which none of them could hope to explain.

She led him through the halls, and out into the greenhouse.

They stood together before the tree, its boughs weighed down with riotous, impossible blooms. Their kin in her throat burned, and she thought she could hear Evelyn whisper, *You are not to blame.*

And then, a little louder,

See how my garden grows.

About the Author

Caitlin Starling is a writer of horror-tinged speculative fiction and interactive media. Her first novel, *The Luminous Dead*, is out now from HarperVoyager. She tweets at @see_starling and has been paid to design body parts. You can find links to her work and ongoing projects at www.caitlinstarling.com.

About the Press

Neon Hemlock is an emerging purveyor of queer chapbooks and speculative fiction. Learn more at www.neonhemlock.com and on Twitter at @neonhemlock.